MARK FERGUSON

Buying Into Success

A fun, thought-provoking journey through life and real estate.

 INVESTFOURMORE

First edition

Editing by Gregory Alan Helmerick

This book was professionally typeset on Reedsy.
Find out more at reedsy.com

Contents

Foreword

I will be completely honest—I was scared to write this book. I am a real estate investor and real estate broker. I have written 6 books on house flipping, rental properties, being an agent, buying a house, negotiating, and how our attitude affects our success.

My previous books have all been non-fiction and were meant to educate those who were already interested in real estate. I taught beginner, intermediate, and advanced techniques, but it is hard to get someone to read a book about rental properties if they do not care about rental properties!

When I think of ways I can make a difference in the world, teaching real estate to those who do not know about real estate always comes to mind first. *Rich Dad Poor Dad* by Robert Kiyosaki is one of the most popular personal finance books in the world, and it includes a story to keep people interested. I knew if I wanted to get more people involved, I would have to write a story, and a fiction one, yikes! This was way out of my comfort zone, but one of the things I love to do is write, and I decided to just go for it.

It took me a long time to write this book. You may notice a Tiger Woods reference that seems outdated, and that's because I first wrote that more than 2 years ago when many people thought Tiger had no hopes of coming back to golf. Now that he has won a major, I thought it would be cool to leave the reference in without changing it.

While *Rich Dad Poor Dad* helped inspire the style of this book, I did not want it to be the same type of book. *Rich Dad Poor Dad* is very motivational and inspiring. I wanted to tell a story about exactly how someone can do what is done in this book. I did not want motivation without direction. This book is about a young adult who learns to buy his first house/investment property. Along the way, I go into the details on real estate agents, loans, finding deals, inspections, appraisals, etc. I talk about flipping vs. renting vs. wholesaling.

I wanted a story that would teach people how wonderful real estate can be and how to actually do it, even if they know nothing about the business (so many people who buy houses know nothing about what they are doing).

I hope you enjoy the story and you find value in this book to give it those who are looking to get ahead in life but may not know how. If you want even more details on how to do what I do, check out my other books on Amazon.

-Mark Ferguson
   -House Flipper (over 175 sold)
   -Owner and Managing Broker Blue Steel Real Estate
   -Rental Property Owner (over 20 properties)
   -Blogger/Youtuber (InvestFourMore)

Dedication

This book is dedicated to everyone who went through our schooling system but received no education on real estate or wealth creation. We are all taught how to get a job, when there is so much more out there.

I

Part One

1

Is this all there is?

Mo was waiting impatiently for his turn to throw three darts. Cory and Rob were playing with him and being extremely slow about taking their turns. They were mostly concerned with checking out a cute blonde sitting at the table beside them. Mo was more concerned with beating them at darts because he was positive that blonde wanted nothing to do with any of them. He was also fairly certain he could wrap this game up on his next turn. Beating them never got old. He could do this all night.

Mo and his buddies were at Burkes, a bar that catered to young adults like Mo, who was 23. The bar was fairly clean but still smelled of beer. Chunky wooden tables were scattered throughout with a few pool tables, dart boards, and video games. The place served food—food that was not going to win any awards—but Mo thought it was decent.

Along one wall was the actual bar, which was about 50 feet long and full of people having a good time. The bar had been well used but was still in good shape. It was a Saturday night, and every table and chair was usually occupied on the weekends. Mo had not doubt that the staff at Burkes was a big reason it was so popular. The servers did their job well, but more than that, they looked like the manager had hand picked them to get the attention of young males. Short shorts were the norm, and Mo never complained about that.

"Take your turn!" Cory yelled at Mo.

Cory was a couple of inches shorter than Mo with very short, blonde hair—almost a buzz cut. He was a pretty strong guy but was cool as hell and would never hurt anyone. You could tell he was an athlete, and he still played basketball and football.

Mo turned around and realized he had been ignoring the game. It must have been his turn for a while. Mo laughed and took the darts, but Cory was not going to let him off that easy.

"This entire game you are telling us to hurry up and take our turn. Then, you aren't even paying attention come your time to throw. How rude. Do you have any idea how that makes us feel?" Cory asked sarcastically. He was kidding around, and Mo loved that about these two. They could joke, laugh, and make fun of each other, and rarely did anyone take anything seriously.

"I was hoping you two would take a few practice turns so I would have some competition," Mo replied quickly. He was partially serious. He was killing them at darts.

Mo, Cory, and Rob finished their game of darts and sat down at a table. Their jackets were hanging on the chairs so no one would think they could snag it. They technically had a server who would stop by the table once in a while, but it was a busy place, and they knew they would get their beer faster at the bar.

Mo went to ask for another pitcher of Coors Light, which they would polish off pretty quickly. He decided he better ask for two more so he would not have to make the trip to the bar again.

4

The rest of the night was uneventful. They drank more beer, played pool, and talked to random friends they knew from the bar scene. They also talked to a girl once in a while.

Around 1 a.m. the bar was starting to shut down, and they knew it was about time to head home. They were all drunk, young, laughing and having a great ol' time. They did not have a care in the world, at least Cory and Rob seemed not to have a care in the world.

Mo was not exactly happy about having to go home. He felt like something was missing from his life, and the bar had not filled the gap yet. Deep down he knew he was partying too much and not taking his life seriously. Things had gone fine for him but definitely not how he had dreamed his life would be when he was younger. He was supposed to be rich and or famous by now.

Where had things gone wrong?

2

Where is all the money?

Mo woke up the next morning groggy, but he didn't feel horrible. He didn't have a splitting headache that everyone in the movies always seemed to have after a night of partying. Maybe he was immune to hangovers, or he was just young enough that they did not affect him much.

He remembered most of the previous night. Before the bar, he had gone to Cory and Rob's house after work. He brought a 30 pack, and they proceeded to drink beer after beer until it got late enough to head to Burkes. Mo loved playing games, and he loved to win.

Before the bars, the guys would play ping pong, darts, card games, or other drinking games. They would watch television and make fun of each other. It was fun, and after the bar, they had headed back to Rob's to play a few more games before Cory walked home and Mo slept on Rob's couch. Mo and his friends made a point never to drive drunk. It was not worth it, and with Uber, they didn't need to drive anyway. Although, enough Uber bills did add up to some serious cash.

Rob was still asleep. He was cool...but quiet. He opened up a lot when he drank but did not say much otherwise. He and Mo had similar statures. They were both about 6 feet tall, worked out once in a while, but were not in amazing shape. Who had time to hit the gym when you worked all week and partied all weekend?

It was 9 a.m. on a Saturday, and Mo didn't have anything to do. He laid on the couch for a while, checking his email on his phone and surfing a few websites like ESPN. It wasn't football season; basketball was over; and the only sports to pay attention to were baseball and golf. He didn't much like baseball, and who gets excited over golf scores? Maybe he would pay attention if Tiger got it going again .

Mo figured he should get home and clean his apartment or do something else useful.

He left the house and got in his 5-year-old Nissan. He liked cars, and the Maxima was affordable, pretty quick, and looked decent. The car was black and suited him well. He would love to get a newer model but could not afford the higher payments.

As Mo drove home, he started to think a little bit about his life. He had graduated high school with decent grades, finished college with mediocre grades, and found a job. He worked for a large insurance company doing IT work. He loved computers but didn't exactly like doing IT work that mostly involved solving extremely simple problems that the office staff managed to come across constantly.

Mo had dated some girls over the years. A few got somewhat serious, but he knew they were not the one. He thought he might meet the girl of his dreams going to bars, but that never seemed to happen. Besides not having a steady girlfriend, Mo realized a few things were wrong with his life.

For one thing, he had a decent job, which his friends told him was a miracle. Then again, his friends weren't exactly trying very hard to

7

find decent jobs and didn't have very many employable skills. They were a blast to play beer pong with though.

Even though everyone told him he was on track at 23 with a decent job, he didn't feel on track—at least—he didn't feel like he was on his track. Maybe he was on someone else's track. Maybe his friends would be happy with his job, but he wanted more. Sure he was young, but he always heard the younger you start investing or building something, the better off you will be.

Mo had no investments. He had no savings account, no stocks, and no IRAs, and he never saved much money. He wasn't really sure what he was on track for because he had nothing to show for a couple years of work and he didn't see any huge promotions in his future. Sure, drinking and partying was fun, but it wasn't always fun the next day, and he didn't seem to be accomplishing much.

So what was he to do?

Mo figured he had to change something if he wanted things to change. He always thought he would find the perfect girl, but lately, he kept meeting girls who weren't interested in partying. At first, this seemed pretty lame to him. Who didn't want to party? They were obviously not the right girl for him.

Then he had a crazy thought. What if drinking all the time was not all there was to life? Sure he had fun, but he wasn't building anything. Sometimes, he did not even remember what was so fun the next morning. He laughed a lot and told a lot of jokes, but nothing meaningful happened.

He had justified this in the past by thinking *I'm still young, I don't have to build anything yet.* When others, especially girls, started to think

8

he wasn't worth the effort, he usually figured there was something wrong with them. They don't understand me; they don't understand my friends; they just aren't right for me. Mo started to question if he was on the right path and whether the problem was with him.

Mo got home and made some breakfast right away. He was starving, and Rob never had any food he could steal. He started to make an omelet with eggs and a little cheese.

While Mo was waiting for the stove to heat up, he had a crazy thought. He Googled "how to get rich" to see what came up. He was surprised by how many results there were. Apparently, a lot of people wanted to know how to get rich!

Mo cracked three eggs into a bowl, whisked them up with a fork, and dumped them into a frying pan with a bunch of oil in it. He began reading a few articles about how to get rich while he waited for the eggs to cook. One article he read said that being rich came from the right attitude about life. "What a load of crap," Mo said out loud. He lived by himself in a one bedroom apartment, and he often talked out loud to himself.

Mo was wondering how a good attitude allowed all the rich dudes to inherit their money. He guessed that their parents would still give them trust funds whether they had an awesome or mediocre attitude. Mo's eggs were ready so he flipped the omelet, only spilling a little egg on his stove, waited a few seconds, and slid it onto a plate where he sprinkled the cheese on half of it then folded the other side onto the cheese.

He flipped on the TV, sat on his couch, and enjoyed the food.

3

An introduction to success

Mo was planning to clean his house, work out, and do a bunch of other meaningful things that day. However, he was tired, hungover, and didn't feel like doing much. Actually, he reminded himself that he was not hungover—that did not happen to him. He was just tired. He ended up lounging around, watching TV, and generally feeling like crap.

When he was finished with a night of partying, he never felt well...not because he physically felt sick, but because he felt useless. He did not want to do anything or get anything accomplished, and it felt like he wasted the day.

After not doing anything all day, he would get anxious and or depressed because nothing was happening. Mo began to realize that nothing was happening a lot. It was not just limited to the days after he drank. He felt like nothing was really happening in his life as a whole. The best way to cheer himself up after he got in this kind of mood was to have a drink!

He knew it was not healthy to drink on a Sunday, by yourself, just because you needed to cheer yourself up. He could call Rob or Cory, and they would hang out with him, but then it would turn into another drink fest. They would go to the bars, and he would be really hungover tomorrow at work. That would not solve any of his issues either: it would just push them off to the next day, but they would be even worse because he would feel even more useless at work.

He would not call Rob or Cory, but he would make himself a rum and coke. After making himself a drink, he decided he would look into some of those articles about making something of your life. He would be taking steps towards improving his life, and at the same time, not be doing anything too strenuous.

Mo found more articles on success and making something of your life. They all had the same theme: change your attitude, work harder than other people are willing to work, and be careful who you hang out with. Mo had the usual reaction to this stuff when he first started reading them. Yeah right. This is just a bunch of BS that doesn't apply to him. Mo was smart. He didn't need this self-help crap. Why did it keep popping up when he was trying to learn how to be rich?

After reading article after article that said similar things, he was beginning to wonder if there was something to any of it.

After reading more articles about making money and different ways to get rich, Mo found something interesting: *Rich Dad Poor Dad*. He remembered hearing about this book before. He had no idea where, but it was familiar.

The book appeared to be about two families, one rich and one poor. The book taught how the poor remained poor and how the rich became and stayed rich. It had a lot of great reviews. Mo read a sample of it online and was surprised how easy it was to read. It also claimed to be the most-read personal financial book of all time. He decided to take a chance and buy the book.

That was enough work for the day.

4

Work

T he next day, Mo felt better about himself. He had taken some action to take control of his life. He hadn't made any big changes, but he had ordered a book.

He went to work that morning, and although he was feeling better about his life, he was just as frustrated at work as he normally was. He realized how much time and talent he was wasting. He knew how to build websites, how to program, and how to solve extremely complicated computer programs. Yet, he spent his time helping clueless insurance drones. He wasn't even helping insurance agents—he was helping the back office staff. Everyone said he had a great job was lucky, but he felt stupid. Why was he working here, under-utilizing everything he knew?

Mo did not work at a small insurance agency but rather the large corporate (or regional...he didn't really care) headquarters for one of the larger companies in the country. The people who worked there consisted of underwriters, actuaries, call-center staff, claims adjusters, and other really boring jobs. At least, that was how Mo looked at all of it.

Mo showed up to work in his Maxima right before 8 a.m. every weekday.

He parked in the lot, which held hundreds of cars, maybe more. He would walk in the building, show his security badge, and walk into his office, which was on the main floor of the two-story building. The building was about 10 minutes from his apartment and was outside of town when it was built 15 year ago. However, the town was starting to catch up to the area, and a few restaurants and other businesses were moving in.

Mo had an office, which was nice, but he shared it with a few other IT guys. The two guys were what Mo would call IT nerds. They had very few social skills and rarely talked to anyone but themselves. They seemed to be obsessed with video games, but Mo had to admit they were good at their jobs.

He had a small desk with a few drawers on one side, a nice laptop, and a filing cabinet. The office had no windows but was close to the coffee station. When he first started at his job, Mo thought being close to coffee was nice. He quickly realized that being close to coffee meant everyone walked by the office, and everyone had to stop in to complain about the latest problem with their computer. It was a never-ending stream of complaints, and if anyone had any real work to do in the room, it was almost impossible to get it done.

Mo had been working there a little over a year. His annual salary was $42,000. His friends thought this was awesome. The had all graduated college a few years ago, but Mo was the only one with a corporate job. Rob was trying to be a stock broker from what Mo could tell. He had gotten a degree in finance but worked for a local investment guy. From what Rob said, he was mostly a secretary and was not learning crap about investing. He got paid $14 an hour and commissions, but he had no clients, so he was not sure how the commissions ever came into play. Cory had gotten a degree in marketing but had no idea what to do with it. He was waiting tables until he found his perfect job.

Mo did not think $42,000 a year was very much, especially after paying his $1,100 monthly rent. He also had to pay for utilities, his phone, cable, food, car payments, and of course going out. Mo's company had a retirement plan with a 401k or something, but Mo did not participate in it. He figured he would rather keep his money.

That day went about as well as it could considering he hated his job. He helped fix about 20 email accounts, and he helped get a few computers back online after they stopped connecting to the WiFi. His boss, Tory, never said much to any of them. The systems they used were antiquated, but Tory did not seem to care. It was all state of the art 15 years ago, but things change quickly with technology. Supposedly, the company was going to upgrade the network, but Mo had no idea when or if that would actually happen.

The clock hit 5 and Mo started to head out of the office with the rest of the company. He did not talk much to anyone and mostly kept to himself at work. He was not excited to be there, but he was excited to leave, that was for sure.

5

Rich Dad

Mo drove home from work, having a little fun in the Maxima. He usually drove a little too fast but never thought much of it. He liked cars and the feeling of acceleration. He knew the Maxima was not the fastest car in the world or close to it, but it was quick.

That night, he didn't go to his friend's house, which he sometimes did during the week. It was a Monday after all! Cory texted Mo asking him if he was doing anything. Cory knew Mo was not doing anything since he did not have a girlfriend or any other people he hung out with. Mo told him he was going to stay in tonight and lied about having a big day at work in the morning. Every day was the same at work. He did not have a big day, but he didn't want to go out either.

He stayed home and cleaned his apartment. He had realized that it was a pigsty, and if he did find the right girl and she decided to visit his place, he would scare her away. It was funny, but just cleaning his apartment made Mo feel better. He felt like he had done something constructive. Plus, having a clean place made him feel better as well. His head felt clear, and he thought he was starting to figure something out. He didn't know what he was figuring out yet, but something good was happening—he knew it.

Mo went through the same routine at work the next day. When he got home, he found his book had arrived. He loved technology and how fast things evolved. It seemed like things were arriving almost the same day you ordered them now.

Mo was excited to read the book but was also a little nervous. What if the book didn't have the answers he was looking for? Honestly, that was not really what he was afraid of. He was afraid that the book would have the answers he wanted, but he would not want to make the changes in his life that would be needed. Could he do it? Would he have what it takes?

Mo began to read and was not disappointed. The book was really good. He read three quarters it the first night.

The drive to work, the walk to his office, and work the next day was the same as it always was. However, he was not quite as upset at work as usual. *Rich Dad Poor Dad* had started to make him think about things. He was not mad at the world or bored out of his mind at work because he was thinking about his life.

The book was very motivational. It discussed two different dads, one who worked for a living his entire life and one who started businesses and invested. The rich dad did not have to work anymore, and the poor dad still worked for someone else and had no end in sight. Rich dad could do whatever he wanted because he invested wisely and built his own businesses...he did not depend on anyone.

The book harped on how investing your money and having your money work for you was the key to success. The key to success was not making as much as you could but saving and then making that money work for you. This was a new concept to Mo. He had never been taught much about financial literacy, even in college. College taught him how to work on computers and how to get a job. It taught him nothing about investing.

The book also talked a lot about real estate and how it could be the best way to invest the money you saved. Mo had always had the idea of buying a house in the back of his mind, but he assumed that would happen when he found a girl, got married, and had kids. He never thought of a house as an investment. After Mo read the book, he was pumped. He knew he wanted to be an investor, not a worker, but he had no idea where to start.

He was hoping the last part of the book would shed some light on what he should do now. He was a bit confused by the book though. It talked a lot about real estate being a good investment, but it also said a house was not a good investment. The two ideas seemed to contradict themselves, but Mo thought he sort of understood what the author was trying to convey.

The idea was that investment properties would produce cash flow or income every month, while a house would produce expenses every month. In fact, the book liked to call a personal house a liability but an investment property that makes money an asset.

Mo had taken some business classes in college, and this is where he was having a hard time grasping the book's concept. He had paid some attention to the accounting class he had taken. They clearly taught an asset was something that you had in your possession, like a house, car, gold bars, etc. A liability was a debt you owed...like the mortgage on the house.

Mo thought he knew what the book was saying: a house is not an asset because it doesn't generate money. Instead, it costs money He was not sure he agreed with the wording, but he could see that a house may not be a great investment for many people.

Mo also thought about his own situation. He had rented his entire life and had nothing to show for all that rent he had paid. He had no equity, no savings, and almost no investments. If buying a house was so bad, renting had not treated him any better. However, he had to admit that he had not tried to learn a thing about getting ahead financially.

He was only partially through the book, but Mo already felt like he had made a turn in his life. He may have more control of his finances than he realized.

6

Money should work for you

The next day, work went the same as it always did, but again, Mo was not quite as mad about his job. Maybe the book or his new outlook had distracted him enough that he could ignore how much he hated work. Thoughts about his finances and life distracted him so much that the day flew by. He could not believe how quickly quitting time came.

Mo headed home and quickly finished the book. Unfortunately, the last part did not tell Mo exactly what to do with his life and how to do it. The book was very motivational, but it left Mo with a lot of questions. It got Mo excited about life and investing, but it did not tell him how to invest or the first step to get started. He still felt like he was on to something and his life was going to get much better from here on out. But, he did not know what to do next.

Rich Dad Poor Dad taught Mo much more about money and how it should always be working for him. He should not be constantly working for money to live on and never making any progress. The book talked a lot about the Rat Race and how people strive to make more and more money. When they make more and more money, they buy more and more stuff. They need more and more money to pay for all the stuff, and it is a constant struggle.

The rich dad in the book owned a lot of real estate and many businesses but had very little education. The book didn't delve into how the rich dad bought the real estate or how he started those businesses, just that he had them, and that eventually made him one of the richest men in Hawaii, where the book was based. Mo thought that was great for the rich dad, but he was not sure how to buy real estate or start a business.

Mo thought the first step in buying real estate was to buy a house to live in, but according to the book, that may be a bad idea. He was not sure what to do. He saw that Robert Kiyosaki, the author of *Rich Dad Poor Dad* had written a lot of books. He decided to order a few more to learn exactly how to invest instead of the basic concept of why he should be investing.

Mo woke up the day after finishing the book energized and ex-cited—until he realized he had to go to work. Work was not fun. It was not investing, and it was not leading anywhere. Mo barely got through work without quitting that day.

He knew this job was wrong. He had ideas and things that could be implemented in the business, but it was clear that his opinion was not needed for business growth. All he could do that day was think about his future and how he had no control over it. At his current job, he was helping someone else make money, and he was barely making enough to get by.

He did not feel lucky at all to have what his friends called a "great job." He felt stuck. Even if he went all out, worked his butt off for years, and managed to get a few promotions, he still would not be close to where he wanted to be. The top managers above him did not make much more money than he did. It seemed the biggest perk of the job was they got to call themselves a manager. The whole corporate environment appeared to be flawed, or at least leaned vastly in favor of the owners of the company. *Rich Dad Poor Dad* was starting to make much more sense now. But how in the world would he be able to start a business or get out of the corporate world?

Mo went home frustrated that day. He sped home in his Maxima, and two blocks before he got to his apartment—boom—red and blue lights. What else could go wrong? He worked hard, paid his bills, was a contributing member of society, and now he was getting pulled over. Yes, he was speeding, but were there not much worse criminal acts being committed at this exact time?

Mo pulled over right away, and the cop came up on his driver's side. Mo had been in a 45 mile per hour zone and was probably going 60 or 65. He was not sure. Mo had learned over the years that being honest with cops usually worked better than BS. Mo turned off his car and rolled down the window. The cop asked Mo if he knew why he pulled him over, and Mo said, "Yes, I was speeding." The cop asked Mo how fast he was going. Mo said, "57 or 58 when I looked at my speedometer."

The cop replied that he clocked him at 62 and asked why he was going so fast. Mo had no good reason for speeding. He said what came to mind.

"I was headed home after a bad day at work and not paying attention."

The cop took his drivers license, insurance, and registration and left Mo to think. The worst part about being pulled over is all the cars passing you. You know they are all thinking how horrible of a person you are and how you got caught being a horrible person. Mo slumped down in his seat a little so he wasn't as visible to those judgmental cars. He waited for the cop, who could have been looking for child molesters or murders.

The cop said he was going to let Mo off with a warning. He appreciated him being honest but that he had to slow down. The cop mentioned something about speeding leading to accidents and accidents being the number one killer of people Mo's age. Mo figured the cop was actually right. He was probably not going to stop speeding because he was an excellent driver, but he thought the police pulling over reckless speeding drivers was not all a huge waste of time.

Mo went home and thought about calling Cory and Rob. It was Friday night, and they would be expecting him to just show up with beer. Mo was not sure if he was in the mood to party. He kind of wanted to learn more about real estate.

Mo stopped himself right there and asked the empty apartment, "What the hell is wrong with me?"

He decided to get some beer and head on over to his friends' place. He needed to relax.

7

Where is the support?

T hat Saturday night, Mo hung out with his friends again, even though he had told himself he wouldn't. He was not just hanging out with them to drink. He also wanted to share some of the things he head learned and what he was thinking about. Mo and his friends did not talk about their feelings, plans, or goals very often. Once in a while, they would talk about their lives and what they wanted to do in the future. None of them had seemed to have very big plans up to this point. At least, none of them wanted to share what their plans or dreams were.

Mo met up with Cory and Rob at Rob's apartment. They had some beers, and Mo told them about the book and how excited he was to start something for himself. Cory flat out said, "You're crazy man. Do you know how many people want to be rich real estate investors or start a business and fail? That is a great way to go bankrupt and lose everything you have."

Mo replied, "I have a decent job, yes, but I hate it. What do I really have to show for my life? I have no savings, no girlfriend, don't own anything that valuable except my car, and I have a loan on that."

Rob chimed in, "You have it so much better than most people. Our jobs suck; we barely can get by. You have a decent apartment and are just starting out with your life. Be thankful!"

This was not going at all how Mo had thought it would. He thought they would be interested and encourage him to better his life. He thought they might even be interested in reading the book. That was clearly not the case. Mo did not bring the subject up again.

They were all getting ready to head to Burke's again when Mo said something that made them all stop in their tracks.

"I don't think I am going to make it to the bar tonight. I am going to call it an early night and head home."

Cory stared at Mo in disbelief. "Is this because of that stupid book?"

Mo replied, "No. I just don't want to get wasted tonight. It makes me feel like crap. I don't even remember what we do, and I have a lot of things to do tomorrow."

Before they could say anything else, Mo walked to his car, got in and headed home.

His friends were really annoyed that Mo had stopped going out with them as much. Instead of partying every weekend and some weeknights, Mo was staying home. His books came a day or two later, and he was obsessed with reading them and learning what to do next.

Mo read every book from Robert he could find, but he did not find what he was looking for. He found more theory and high-level ideas but few details on how to get started. Mo was getting frustrated, but knew he could not give up.

After reading another Kiyosaki book, Mo decided to do some searching online. What he found was Kiyosaki offered a real estate coaching program. Now he was pumped. He would get the help he needed. Mo read a lot about real estate in the books but wasn't sure where to start or how to go about it. He rented a place by himself and never even thought he was in a position to buy a house.

Mo found a three-day seminar that was only an hour away from him, and he signed up immediately.

8

The seminar

M o could not wait for the seminar. He started to do a little research online about Rich Dad coaching and loved what he saw from the description. He found a few naysayers on other websites, but he was used to that. His friends had shown him how discouraging people who had no idea what they were talking about could be.

In fact, he was drifting further and further away from his friends. They kept pressuring him to go out and party, but Mo was too excited about creating his future and building something with his life. He really had nothing to show for all his hard work. He couldn't really remember what was so fun about going out all the time. Yes he knew he had fun and laughed, but the memories all involved drinking. He did not have many deep connections, and every time he woke up, he felt like something was missing. Sure, he had a good time, but he couldn't remember half of the fun he had.

When Mo read some of the websites, they said Rich Dad coaching was a ripoff and too expensive, but he knew he needed someone to teach him the details of how to get ahead. He needed more than high-level ideas. He did not pay too much attention to what those sites were saying. He needed to see what this was all about for himself.

As the date for his seminar came closer, Mo was nervous, excited, and could not sit still. He knew his work was suffering because he could not concentrate. He kept thinking about a better life and a better future. The sad thing was, no one at work seemed to notice he wasn't working as hard or was as committed. He got his work done, but his heart was definitely not in it. To be honest, his heart was never in it, but it was even less in it now. He started to wonder how little he could do and still get paid!

Mo kept working, but all he could think about was starting his own business and not working for someone else. He kept getting paid for what he thought was mediocre work. He was barely even thinking about his job because his seminar was tomorrow. Mo had taken off work to attend the seminar (it was on a Friday afternoon, and he had plenty of vacation time saved up).

That Saturday, he woke up early, gathered his things—phone, charger, notebook, pen, his Rich Dad book—and waited. The seminar was not for a few more hours. Mo was ready to learn how to take control of his life, and now he had to wait.

He messed around in his apartment and had an idea. He would work out! It had been months since the last time he did any real physical activity. He changed clothes, did some push ups, sit-ups, squats, and curls with some dumbbells he found sitting in the back of his closet. He felt so good! And, he still had plenty of energy to spare.

It was about time to leave for the Rich Dad seminar, so he showered, changed, and headed out the door. He got to his car and remembered he left all his stuff in the apartment. He ran back to get it and headed out.

Mo arrived at the event center with a couple hundred other people. He was hoping he would meet Robert Kiyosaki and be able to express how much his books had meant to him. Mo found a seat and was sweating because he was so nervous, even though it was actually quite cold in the room. He even sat in the front of the room, although in school, he was always as far away from the teacher as possible.

The seminar started with stories about success and those who had found success with the program. The seminar talked about how much money real estate investors could make and how seemingly easy it was. Mo was pumped. He knew he was going to get the goods soon and figure out what his next step were.

As the seminar progressed, Mo was getting more nervous...or maybe anxious. There was more talk about making money and more success stories, but he was not getting any details. The seminar felt like the books he read: great for motivation but short on specifics.

Robert was nowhere to be found, and they said he would not be making it to this seminar. That certainly sucked. Mo was looking forward to learning from him and maybe even shaking his hand. That was one of the main reasons he decided to go.

At the end of the seminar, Mo was hit what felt like a Mack truck. They wanted $1,200 to get the real Rich Dad training at a 3-day seminar. They even mentioned something about a fast-track mentoring program that probably cost even more money.

A few people started to get in line to talk to people about signing up for the coaching. Mo was in front and overheard some of the salesman trying to convince people to call their banks to raise their credit card limits or call relatives to borrow money for the training. The fast track training was $30,000! This was exactly how the websites that warned Mo about the seminar said it would play out.

Mo would be lying if he said he was not seriously thinking about signing up. He could not ever fathom paying that much for a real estate program, but they made it seem so easy, and he knew he needed coaching to get where he wanted to be. Mo was thinking about his finances and knew there was no way he could pay $30,000. $1,200 would even be a huge stretch for him. Even though he knew he needed help, it was simply impossible. The seminar speakers said he had to sign up that day or the price would go up, but he simply could not do it. He also hated being pushed into buying something with used-car-salesman tactics.

He went home disappointed, confused, and a little empty. The seminar had not gone how he imagined it, and he did not feel any more educated. Maybe Rich Dad was not the program for him. He was still motivated, and it would take a lot more than this to make him give up. However, he was hugely disappointed.

9

Research research research

Mo tried not to focus on the real estate/business ideas. He thought hard about what to do. He could ask his parents for money...or his friends (yeah right they had no money). He could raise his credit card limits and just go for it. But, he just could not justify spending that much money at this point in his life.

He decided to stop thinking about it. He went out with his friends, had fun, and relaxed. He talked to his buddies about the seminar, and they told him he was wasting his time. They were not mean about it, but they weren't encouraging either. He had a great night and probably drank too much, stayed up too late, and ate too much food at a late-night diner they sometimes went to after the bar. In the morning, Mo still had that empty feeling. Going out was fun, but he also knew that was not the lifestyle he wanted every night—or even a few nights a week. He decided it was time to try something new. He would read other books and websites and learn what real estate investing was all about.

He searched for more books and articles on real estate investing. He found so many books that he had a hard time deciding what he even wanted to concentrate on. The seminar he went to focused on flipping houses, which seemed cool. However, there were books on being a real estate agent, rental properties, buying with no money down, and wholesaling. He did not even know what wholesaling was! He found a book by Gary Keller called *Millionaire Real Estate Investor*. It had a lot of great reviews and was written by the guy who started Keller Williams. He thought that gave the guy a lot of credibility, and he didn't want to get sucked into another seminar trap.

While he waited for the book, he decided to research some of the topics the other books he found covered. He started with real estate agents. He had heard of them, obviously, but never really knew how they made money or what they did. Some agents seemed to make a ton of money on TV, but he also knew a friend of a friend who was an agent, and she gave up the business in less than a year. She had told everyone it was a horrible business to be in, and it was impossible to make money. In the past, Mo would have let that stop him, but he was realizing that most people he knew, and maybe most people in general, were very negative. Everyone seemed to complain about everything and how unfair life was. Maybe life was not unfair because of things that happen to you but because of the choices you make. Mo had seen his friends, who he thought would be interested and encouraged by his new ideas, be completely discouraging.

Mo found a few articles about how much money real estate agents make. It was a little depressing seeing that the average salary for agents was in the $30,000 to $40,000 range. That was less than he made now. Some of the articles mentioned that being an agent had its perks, like being your own boss and making your own schedule. That seemed like it would be nice, but then Mo saw what agents make in their first year. Some sites said it was less than $10,000 and suggested new agents save up 6 months of living expenses before they started. That was crazy! How can anyone save that much money just so they can make $10,000 their first year and maybe work up to $40,000? That seemed like a horrible career. He decided he had read enough about real estate agents.

The next subject Mo researched was wholesaling. He had no idea what wholesaling was, so he thought it would be interesting to at least see what the term meant. He searched a few times and kept ending up getting invited to a webinar to learn how to make millions wholesaling. He was not interested in a webinar. He just wanted to know what wholesaling meant!

Finally, he found a site that gave him some information on what wholesaling is. From what Mo could gather, wholesaling was when an investor got a house under contract and sold it to another investor without doing any work. He was not sure what "under contract" meant exactly, but he thought it had something to do with buying a house. A lot of sites mentioned how you can make millions wholesaling real estate without using any of your own money. This sounded great, but again, Mo was skeptical that they just wanted his $30,000. Wholesaling still sounded interesting to him, so he dug into more and more articles.

He began to get a clearer idea of the concept. A real estate investor would try to find an awesome deal by looking for houses that were not for sale. They were like the We Buy Ugly Houses people. They put up banners and signs, looked for run-down houses, and tried to get the owners to sell the houses for pennies on the dollar. Once the investor found a house to buy, they would get a contract signed with the owner (that was what under contract meant). The investor would then find another investor to sell the house to for more money than the first investor bought it for. The first investor or wholesaler made the difference in the two prices as the wholesale fee. The concept seemed simple enough, but the execution seemed really complicated.

How could he find these houses so cheap?

What would he say to the sellers to get them to sell?

Where would he get a contract?

Was this even legal?

How would he find the buyers for these houses and convince them it was a good deal?

What if he could not find any buyers?

Did he need a real estate license to do this?

He figured he had learned enough about wholesaling and real estate agents for one night and went to bed.

10

Are rentals the asnwer?

Mo woke up tired the next day. He did not go to bed until 2 a.m. and had to be to work at 8. Luckily his job took almost no brain cells. He spent most of his morning convincing Sarah in accounting that she did not need to send $200 in bitcoin to a random person who emailed her claiming to have photos of her. He got through the day, but it was getting tougher and tougher. He hated his job, and knew there were better things out there for him. He was excited about real estate, but also knew he had so much to learn. Thinking about how long it might take him to actually buy a house, let alone an investment property, frustrated him. He even started thinking about the $30,000 seminar and if he should work on a goal of saving up that money. In the end, he decided to stop feeling sorry for himself. If he wanted his life to change, he would have to plug along until he changed it.

After work, Mo really wanted his new book to come, but he knew it would be a day or two. He thought about calling his friends to go out but decided to keep working on his new found passion. Well, he didn't really know what his passion was, but he was excited and motivated. He just needed to learn what to be excited and motivated about! Mo got to work researching more topics on his computer. He started to look into rental properties.

The concept behind rental properties was interesting. He had always assumed that really rich people bought rental properties with cash and made money from the rent they received. They got richer and bought more rental properties. He was learning that normal people could buy rentals as well, and a lot of websites claimed it was a great way to quit your job, retire early, yada yada yada. He had heard all this before on other sites that promised a lot of money with little work, but you had to buy their program or go to their webinar to actually learn how to do it. However, Mo was beginning to see the difference between the pure marketing sites and the sites that had some information in them. It wasn't all bad out there on the interwebs.

The more Mo researched rental properties, the more he liked the concept. It was also easier to understand and visualize than wholesaling. He learned that you don't have to pay for rentals with cash. You could get investment property loans or even turn a house you lived in into a rental. When you turned a house you lived in into a rental, it took very little money. He learned that in many parts of the country, people pay much more in rent than what a mortgage would be. You did not have to buy a rental property with cash to make money with it. He also learned that rentals benefited from good tax treatment from the government. You could depreciate them and deduct interest on them. He wasn't sure what that meant yet, but it sounded good to him. He found one site that loved to talk about buying properties below market value. This was especially interesting to Mo.

Mo had thought you bought a house for what it was worth. You find a real estate agent; they help you find a house you like; you buy it; and boom—you own a house. You live there for a while, pay down the mortgage, hope the house goes up in value, and boom—you are a homeowner. It seems there was much more to buying a house than what Mo thought.

The concept of buying a house below market value got stuck in his head. Now he knew what the wholesalers were doing. They were buying houses for much less than they were worth, and that is why other investors were willing to buy them for more money. That same concept was not just good for wholesaling but could be used for rental properties. He even read where someone got a great deal on a rental, fixed it up, rented it, and then refinanced the property to get all of their money back out. That sounded amazing but also a little to good to be true.

Mo was excited. He was starting to understand real estate a little more. Rental properties made more sense to him than being an agent or wholesaling. He knew he was a long way off from being a real estate magnate, but he felt a lot better than he did earlier in the day. Now, he really wanted that book to come!

11

Could he flip houses?

Mo was back at work the next day, but it was not as bad as usual. He was feeling better about his life and received fewer questions from colleagues who knew nothing about computers. To be honest, the people who knew nothing were not that bad—it was the people who knew just enough to destroy their computers that were the worst. They thought they knew enough to fix issues on their own yet usually just made things worse. Mo, realized he was getting negative again and decided to stop thinking about how horrible work was. He made money, had a job, and did not have to work outside baking in the summer or freezing in the winter. Before work ended, Sarah had another problem with her email.

Sarah was a little older than Mo and had been in the office a couple of years longer. Mo knew she was in accounting but did not know what that meant exactly. He saw her quite a bit as she always seemed to have a simple problem that needed fixing or a question about something.

Mo thought she was decent looking. She had shoulder length blonde hair, was about 5' 8", slim, but not super skinny, and liked to smile a lot. Mo had tried his best not to get interested in anyone at work, and Sarah was no exception. He also thought she might be a little too boring for him. He just assumed that anyone who was an accountant didn't know how to have fun. He knew how to have fun, although maybe that was changing.

Sarah said hi to Mo when he got close to her cubicle. Most of the office was cubicles with only a few private offices for the managers. Mo said hi back and asked what the issue was.

"My email kicked me out again, and I can't reset my password."

This happened all the time. The office used old systems and equipment, which meant things did not work like they should. Upgrading every-thing would be really easy, but management did not want to spend the money.

Mo was able to log in to the master system on his laptop and reset her password for her. Sarah thanked him and apologized for bothering him again. Mo said, "No problem" and headed back to his shared office. Mo was not as annoyed as he usually was. It really was not the employees' fault they had so many computer problems. Those problems gave him a job. Oh well. Mo packed up and headed home.

At home, Mo dove right back into his research. His book had not come yet, but he was learning how to find good information online. He could learn a lot if he looked in the right places and listened to the right people. Today, he was going to learn about house flipping. He left this subject for last because he was the most excited about it in the beginning. Although, rentals had opened his eyes to real estate investing, he still wanted to learn about flipping. Flipping was sexy, and house flippers always seemed to have Lamborghinis or Ferraris. Mo liked cars, but he never actually thought he would own a Lambo. House flipping was also what the seminar he attended seemed to be about, although they never got into much detail about anything.

Mo thought he knew what house flipping was about. You buy a house, fix it up, and sell it. The concept seemed easy enough. What he did wonder was if these house flippers all made so much money, why didn't everyone do it? Mo thought, *I guess I never did it or researched it myself so that might be one reason.*

Mo realized that most people don't take the time to learn new things or do things that might take them out of their comfort zone. He was going to change that. It might not be today or tomorrow, but eventually, Mo would get out of his dead end job and make some real money. He thought real estate might be the best way to do it.

Mo learned that house flipping was not as easy as they made it seem on TV. The key to flipping was getting good deals. Again, it was the same concept as with rentals and wholesaling. You don't make your money fixing a house. You make your money getting a great deal. Although often, you can get a great deal because a house needs a lot of work.

Mo also learned that finding the money to start is not easy. Most banks do not like to lend to real estate investors. He also learned that flipping a house can take some time. It does not happen in a few weeks or even a few months. Even with financing, it takes a lot of money. Mo was not surprised. He knew that house flipping was not a magical money making machine that would be easy for anyone.

He learned more from the few articles he read on flipping than he did at the seminar he attended. The seminar was all fluff and motivation. He liked the motivation, and it helped him get to where he was today, but he realized he dodged a big bullet when he decided spending $30,000 on coaching was impossible.

House flipping seemed cool, and he was excited about it, but he was not sure how he could start anytime in the near future. He needed money and a lot more knowledge on how to repair houses. Mo thought that rentals may be what he wanted to do, but again, he needed to learn a lot more!

Hopefully, his new book would be here tomorrow.

12

Work is what you make of it

The next day at work, Mo felt even better. He was finding a direction for his life. He had a very fuzzy path, but at least he had a path to follow. The weird thing was, he was starting to hate his job less. He had learned so much about real estate in a few short days, but he also learned how much he didn't know. He learned that there was a lot more to real estate than what you see on TV or what people are taught in school.

He looked at some of his co-workers and realized they don't know anything about computers. They are in the insurance business. They did not go to school to learn about computers. Many of them did not graduate from college, and they have no interest in computers. Mo had no interest in real estate a few weeks ago, and he knew nothing about it. Why was he getting mad at everyone for not knowing as much about computers as he did when that was his job. In fact, if they knew as much about computers as he did, he would not have a job!

While Mo was researching real estate, he had run into some self-help concepts as well. He noticed a lot of the successful people online loved to talk about being positive, working on yourself, and taking responsibility for your actions. Every site he went to seemed to mention your attitude was important. Maybe it was not all BS.

Mo realized right then that he actually was doing some of these things himself already. He had taken action to learn a knew concept. He had taken action to change his life. Maybe there was something to all these successful people using the same techniques and attitudes to be successful.

Mo realized something else at work—when he was more positive and helpful, he had more fun. The day went by faster, and he realized some of the people at work may even be fun to talk to. He started interacting with everyone at work a little more. He talked to Tory more, talked to other people he saw in the office when getting coffee, and even talked to the guys he worked with in the IT room. He would need to learn their names eventually.

When Mo had more fun at work, it made him feel so much better about life. It was such a drag dreading the drive to work and sitting there waiting for the clock to hit that magical time when he could go home. He had a lot more control over his job than he thought. He could make his day more fun or interesting. He could do a little more around the office to make it interesting for other people. He had plenty of time to work on things when he was not fixing tech problems.

He knew the office could benefit from many upgrades on the tech side, but he had not talked to Tory about it much. He had briefly mentioned it a few times, and Tory had not seemed very interested. He mentioned they did not have the money for upgrades and they needed to make due with what had worked for the last 15 years.

The tricky thing about Tory was he was not a tech guy. He understood computers and was smart, but he was not at the level Mo was...or the other IT guys for that matter. He was not sure how Tory had become the manager of the IT department, but it was not for his computer background or knowledge. Mo realized this was something else that had been bothering him about work. How could they hire a guy like Tory when he did not know that much about his department?!

Mo had an idea that was brewing in his head. He had never given any details to Tory about upgrading the office, and Tory probably had no idea what it would take. Maybe he could put some kind of proposal together to show him the costs and benefits of upgrading this place.

If he had a project that challenged him, work would be much more fun and interesting. He might even enjoy it.

13

Millionaire real estate investor

When Mo got home from work, his book had arrived. He was just as excited to read it as he was a few days ago. He had learned a lot online but really want to read a book that talked about the same concepts in detail. It was too easy to get distracted and lose your train of thought reading articles all day.

While there was a lot of good information online, there was also a lot of bad information. There was also a lot of conflicting information. It was also easy to get caught in a rabbit hole chasing article after article without finding exactly what you needed. He was happy to be able to read a cohesive book from one author.

The Millionaire Real Estate Investor was a great book. It was a little old, and some of the concepts seemed outdated from what Mo had learned online, but he still loved the book. It mapped out exactly how real estate investing could change your life. It gave examples of exactly how to do it, and it even had case studies on others who had success with real estate investing. The book was focused on rental properties, which is what Mo thought he should focus on as well. He had learned that it is good to focus on one concept first before he jumped into something else.

While Mo had felt he had learned a lot from his online research and the books he had read, he still felt like he was a long way off from doing any type of investing. He had no money saved, knew nothing about his real estate market, knew no one in the real estate industry, and a change to any of this seemed a long way off.

Mo was getting down on himself. He realized that it had only been a few weeks since he started this journey. He had accomplished a lot, and he was proud of himself for getting as far as he had. It was more fun to learn and be excited about something that could actually change his life.

Still, the question of how he could really start doing this popped into his head. He had learned that he wanted to invest in rentals. He had learned why rentals can be such an awesome investment.

If he bought the right rental property, it would cash flow right away. That meant the rent would cover all of the expenses including a mortgage and still make him money every month.

He learned that most people underestimate the expenses on a rental property. He had to take into account the property taxes, insurance, mortgage, paying a property manager if he had one (if not, he had to account for his own time), maintenance, and vacancies. Most people assumed their rentals would never be vacant and never need any work, but that was not true. Every house will need work no matter how great the tenant is, and every house will eventually have vacancy costs when a tenant moves out.

If Mo used a mortgage to buy a rental, he would be paying down the loan every month. Mo knew he would need to get a loan as he did not have $100,000 in cash lying around. He was not sure if he would ever have that much money lying around. He had always heard how bad debt is, but with real estate, many people seemed to like debt. It was a difficult concept for him to accept because he had been taught how bad debt was his entire life. After learning about rentals and real estate, he was starting to accept that debt could be a good thing.

He would also be able to deduct the interest on the loan as a business expense. He would be able to deduct or depreciate almost all of the other expenses on a rental as well. He also was able to depreciate the value of the structure of the rental. He was not quite sure how that worked, but it sounded like a rental could actually make money but show as a loss on taxes. Maybe this is why people always said real estate was a great tax shelter.

The big thing that Mo learned was that you can buy real estate below market value. That is why getting a loan on a rental is not that risky if you do it the right way. When you buy a house for 20% less than it is worth, you have built-in equity. When you have a house that cash flows you, have money paying all the expenses and some left over. There is still risk when investing in rentals, but they were not as risky as Mo thought they would be, at least when you buy right. If you go out and buy any old house that loses money, you are asking for trouble.

14

Figuring out a path

Mo liked the idea of rental properties the best. He thought he understood how the other techniques worked, but they seemed more like a job than investing. If you flip a house, you have to keep flipping houses over and over to continue to make money. The same goes for being a real estate agent and wholesaling. However, you kept rentals, which meant they kept working for you as long as you owned them.

Mo read the Gary Keller book, ordered more books, and kept reading articles, After a couple of weeks of learning, Mo found another educational channel: YouTube. There were so many real estate investing videos! He had to be careful again with what channels he watched as many of them were marketing and nothing else. There were also some really good videos and channels that taught you all about real estate investing. Mo like to read, but it was also nice to see exactly what people were doing and what the houses looked like in videos. He could start to visualize what type of house he wanted and what he would do to it.

Mo became more confident in his real estate investing endeavor, but he was still a long way from actually doing it. He was hung up on how he would get the money to buy a rental, how he would convince a lender to give him a loan, and how to even find properties that would be great deals. He was not looking for a house to live in. He was looking for an investment!

He started to research strategies that would allow someone to invest in rental properties with little money down. He found a lot of information, and most of it seemed very complicated. He could find a partner who would lend him money; he could ask for seller financing; he could somehow buy a house and then refinance it to get money back; or he could buy as an owner occupant.

The tough part about buying as an owner occupant was Mo did not want to wait a year or two to start earning income on his property. He still had it in the back of his head that buying a house to live in was not a good investment. There was a lot of talk on YouTube and online about living in a house for a short time to get the low down payment loan and then renting out the house. This seemed like a decent plan, and he would have another purpose for the house than living in it for the rest of his life. If he waited until he had 20 or 25 percent to put down on a rental property, it might take him 10 years at the rate he was saving!

If he bought as an owner occupant, he was supposed to live there at least a year before he could rent it out. While it would be tough to wait, Mo realized that he would still be well ahead of where he was now. He had not even thought about buying a house at this point in his life, and now he was thinking of not only buying a house to live in but also buying a house that would become an investment property.

Mo knew he had to start taking some kind of action if he wanted things to keep progressing. He could read articles and watch videos all day long. Articles and videos were educational, but they were not the real world. He needed to get out there in the world and start doing something—anything—to build on what he had learned.

15

New friends

The next Monday, Mo realized that things were getting even better at work. When he enjoyed helping others and realized that not everyone knew as much about computers as he did, he had more fun. He talked to more people at work, and they seemed to talk to him more. He eventually got along well enough with a few people to call them friends. Mo still hung out with Corey and Rob once in a while, but it was rare. Every time he would see them, they wanted to get hammered. He still liked to drink once in a while, but he did not see the point in getting so drunk that you could not walk or socialize. Wasn't that the point of drinking—to have a good time, loosen up, and meet people?

As Mo was packing up for the day, a few co-workers gathered around the coffee room, and Mo could tell they were talking about him. They were discussing something, laughing, and glancing in his direction. Mo was thinking they had a problem that he would need to fix right when he was ready to leave. Maybe things were not getting better.

Jesse, one of the guys Mo had chatted with more at work walked in Mo's direction, and Mo was waiting to hear about whatever problem he had that was sure to need to be solved right now as he was trying to get home.

"Hey Mo, how was your day?" Jesse said with a smile.

"It was alright. No major fires to put out." Mo responded.

"A few of us are going to the new restaurant they just opened down the street. We usually grab a drink before heading home on Mondays. Helps the week go by a little quicker. Do you want to join us?

Mo was not expecting that. It took him a second, but he agreed. Talk about a 180. He was getting ready to fix a computer, and now he was going to hang out. That had worked out well!

Mo headed out with Jesse, who was an underwriter, Thomas, who did something somewhere in the company, and Jeff, who Mo thought was an accountant. They were all a little older than Mo, but none of them were over 30.

They walked over to a restaurant that was about three blocks from the company. It was very modern with an industrial theme to it. They had a patio, and the group grabbed a table. The place was a little different than Burke's. It did not smell of beer. They had no pitcher or keg specials, and there was no darts. Mo knew he would kill these guys at darts. Oh well.

The mood of the restaurant set the scene for the night. Mo was amazed at how different it was compared to hanging out with his friends. They had dinner, a few drinks, went to a bar, where they had a few more drinks, and they all went home. Jesse said they usually did not go to a bar after the restaurant, but it was a special night since they had met a new friend in Mo.

Mo thought it was nice to go out when it was not a contest to see who could stay up the latest before passing out. They were not chugging beers, playing beer pong, or doing more drinking than talking. It was a lot of fun, and Mo learned a lot about the company as well as these new friends.

Mo saw Sarah at the restaurant as well. She also had gone out with a group of co-workers. Apparently, there was an entirely different social system built around this company that Mo was not aware of. He assumed everyone hated their job as much as he did and could not wait to get home after work.

Sarah came over to Mo and seemed super surprised to see him. He did not know why he never paid much attention to her before. It could have been because he was so unhappy at work all the time or because of what he used to think were her stupid questions about her email. She was cute and apparently did not have a boyfriend. They chatted for a while, but the two groups went their separate ways after a few minutes, and they said their goodbyes.

When Mo got back to his apartment, he reflected on the night out. He had fun and felt really good about himself. He met new people or at least got to know people he had worked with much better. They seemed decent and had decent jobs, although most of their jobs seemed very boring. He even mentioned his real estate ambitions to Sarah, and she didn't laugh at him or tell him he was wasting his time. She said she knew a couple of real estate investors through the company, and they seemed to do very well financially.

Mo was encouraged in more ways than one and decided he was definitely on the right track.

16

Enough research

It had been a few weeks since Mo had hung out with the people from work. He went out with them once in a while and had a good time talking and relaxing after work. It was super low key, and he enjoyed having fun without going crazy. He still talked with Sarah once in a while, but he was not pushing anything with her or anyone at the moment. He was concentrating on real estate and learning as much as he could. His job was about the same—he was enjoying it more, but there was still no challenge for him.

He still thought about going above and beyond by presenting Tory with some options for upgrading the system, but he had not done that yet. Maybe soon.

Slowly, Mo was learning more and more about real estate, but it was time for him to take action. He was not ready to buy anything yet, but he was ready to get out of the learning phase. He had been reading books and articles for a couple of months, and he knew he had to do more than learn if he was actually going to do this.

From the books he had read he knew many people got hung up in the learning phase. They would keep reading and learning but never actually do anything with what they had learned. This was often called analysis paralysis. Mo was not going to get stuck in the learning phase.

Luckily, the books had taught him a few thing he could do to take action without actually buying a house. He knew they would be easy to do, but he was still nervous.

He needed to talk to a lender about getting a loan.

He needed to talk to a real estate agent or at least go see some houses.

He did not want to talk to a lender because he was afraid what they would say about him. He had a decent job, but he had never talked to a lender before. What if they told him he could never get a loan?! He knew they would not say that, but he was still scared. One thing that was encouraging him, though, was he was starting to save money. He did not do it on purpose, but by slowing down his partying, he was spending a lot less. He did not realize how much he was spending on alcohol, bars, and late-night food.

He was scared to view houses because the real estate agents may see how little he actually knows and not take him seriously. Again, he knew this was not a valid fear, but he was still scared. He knew if he wanted to change his life, he would have to do some things that he did not want to do. He really did want to see some houses, so he knew he had to get over this fear and do it sooner rather than later.

Mo felt like this was a pivotal point in his life. He was at a crossroads where he could keep learning and going with the flow, and maybe someday, he would buy a house or take some action.

Or, he could take a stand and take action now. He had nothing to lose by taking action. The worst thing that could happen was some people that he never met before did not take him seriously. Even if that did happen, he could just keep searching until he found people who would.

He decided to look at some houses as soon as he could. This weekend, he would visit some open houses, talk to some agents, and then figure out how to talk to a lender.

17

Time to take action

Mo looked on Zillow for houses for sale in his area. He found a number of houses for sale, and a few seemed like decent deals, but he did not see anything spectacular. He really did not know what he was looking for yet. He supposed the perfect house would not be sitting there waiting for him to buy it the first day he started looking.

He found a spot where he could see upcoming open houses and thought that was a better option than bothering a real estate agent. He picked a few properties to visit over the next weekend.

Mo could not believe how nervous he was once he had decided to take some action. Everything became much more real to him. *This real estate thing might actually happen*, he kept thinking to himself. It was a couple of days until the weekend when he was planning to see the open houses. He was a mess at work and could barely concentrate on anything. He managed to get through the days, and finally, Saturday was nearly here. He realized how ironic it was that he was looking forward to Saturday so he could go to open houses by himself. Usually, he was excited for the weekend because he could stay out all night and not have to worry about work in the morning.

Saturday morning came, and he was so worried what the real estate agents would think of him. What if there were other buyers at the houses—or worse yet—other investors? He had no idea what to say to the agents. He thought they would think he was too young. He was worried that he would say something that made no sense to them. He knew he had to do it, so he thought of ways he could make it easier on himself. He would write out some questions to ask the agent once he got to the open house!

Mo wrote a few things down and felt instantly better. He also thought if he had a notepad and pen with him when he looked at the houses, he may look like he knew what he was doing.

Here are some of the questions he jotted down:

What would the house would rent out for?

What do the utilities cost?

Is it in a good area for rental properties?

Are the schools good?

Is it in a high-crime area?

What did the real estate agent think of rentals?

Mo got up his nerve and drove to the first open house on his list. When he was a block away, he saw the open house directional sign, and when he got to the property there was a for sale in the yard, right next to the open house sign. There were no cars parked on the street and an SUV parked in the driveway.

The neighborhood was full of 1970s style ranch homes. Most of them looked exactly the same, well not exactly, but very similar. There were large trees in most of the yards, and there were sidewalks, gutters, and a paved street. It was a very normal and boring neighborhood.

The house was a 1970s brick ranch with a one-car garage. It looked decent from the outside and was very similar to every other house on the street. He noticed the yard was well maintained, although one of the neighbor's yards was dead. He wondered how much the neighbor's house looking like crap would affect the value of this house.

He walked up to the door, which was open, and his stomach churned and his body was full of anxiety. He knocked on the door hesitantly and then walked into the house. No one was in sight. He said hello (rather meekly) and heard a hello back as a thirty-something agent walked in from another room to greet him. The agent was clean cut and wore a dress shirt and dress pants with nice shoes. The agent asked Mo how he was doing and told him to take a look at the house. The agent told Mo if he had any questions to let him know. Mo was expecting to get bombarded with questions from the agent, but it appeared he was going to be able to check out the house on his own.

Mo had his list of questions but decided to tour the house before he asked the agent anything. The agent seemed to be more interested in his phone than Mo anyway.

The house was in really good shape. The front door opened up into the living room where there were hardwood floors, what looked like new paint, and newer lights. The dining room was just back of the living room and connected to the kitchen. There was more hardwood, more new paint, and a bright newer kitchen. Mo was surprised how nice the home looked. It appeared to be completely remodeled. He toured the rest of the house, which had a finished basement, 4 bedrooms, and

2 bathrooms. He saw the basement last, and when he came back up the stairs, he was ready to ask the real estate agent some questions. The agent was still buried in his phone and did not look up when Mo walked up to him.

Mo lost his nerve and decided to walk on by and go to the next house. As Mo got to the front door, the agent finally asked him what he thought of the house. Mo said it was nice, but he had just started looking at houses. The agent asked him what type of house he was looking for, and Mo said he wan't sure yet. The agent asked Mo if he was working with another real estate agent, and Mo said no. The agent then asked if Mo had talked to a lender yet. Mo was not ready for all of these questions! He told the agent he had not talked to a lender yet, but he planned to soon.

The agent was very nice and gave Mo his card. He asked for Mo's phone number and email address, and that was when Mo decided to ask the agent some questions.

"I guess I do have some questions. What do you think this house would rent out for?"

The agent hesitated, and after a few seconds said, "I am not really sure. I specialize in selling homes, and I don't ever get asked to rent them. Are you looking for an investment property or a house to live in?"

Mo replied, "I want to live in the house first, and then rent it out when I move in a year."

The agent said, "I don't think you can do that. When you get an owner-occupied loan, you have to live in the house. Maybe if you refinanced your loan, you could rent it out."

Mo was a bit shocked at that statement. Everything he had ready said he could rent out the home once he had lived there for a year. Now this agent was telling him otherwise. Were the laws different here? Mo wanted to leave and crawl back to his apartment, but he decided to tough it out.

"Do you know how much the utilities are?"

The agent replied, " I don't have that information with me, but you can call the utility companies and ask them."

Mo asked another questions, "Is this a good neighborhood?"

The agent looked really uncomfortable with that question and answered, "Every neighborhood is different for every person. I would not know if this is a good neighborhood for you or not."

Mo was not getting much information, but he kept trying , "Is this a high-crime area?"

The real estate agent looked even more uncomfortable and answered, "I really don't know, but you can look up crime rates online or ask the local police."

Mo was not learning much from the agent, so he asked him one more question, " Do you think this property would make a good rental?

The agent replied, "I don't see why not. The house is in great shape, ready to move into, and there are some other rentals in the area."

Mo was not convinced the agent knew what he was talking about since he didn't even know what the place would rent out for. Mo thanked the agent for his time and walked out the door. The agent did not ask for his email or phone number this time.

18

Finding the right help

Mo left the open house feeling better about some things and worse about others. He was pretty sure he knew more about rental properties than the real estate agent did, and he had just started learning about them a few months ago. Mo was worried about what the agent had said about the loan and turning the house into a rental. However, he wanted to confirm that information with some other agents before he freaked out.

Mo was also depending on real estate agents to help him navigate some of the hurdles he knew he would come up against as a new investor. That agent did not seem to know much about anything. How could he not know if this was a high crime area?

Mo also knew that property would not make a good rental, at least not for him. It was in perfect shape and priced at the top of the market at $179,900, but Mo was looking for something more like the neighbors house that had the dead yard.

Mo saw a couple more open houses and had mostly the same experience. The real estate agents did not know much about rentals. They would tell Mo nothing about the neighborhood or crime rates, and they didn't really know what the houses would rent out for. Mo decided to check out one more house before he got some dinner and headed home.

The next house was in good shape as well. The agent let him walk through the house like the other agents had, and then Mo started to talk to him. Mo was much more comfortable around agents after he realized he knew more about investing than just about all of them. As soon as he started to talk to this agent, he knew he was different. He knew all the answers except for the ones they could not legally answer. When he asked what the crime rate was, the agent said that licensed agents could not legally tell him, that he had to research that information on his own along with how good the schools were. That seemed a little silly to Mo, but it made sense now that the other agents avoided those questions.

Mo asked the agent what they thought the rent would be on this house. He said anywhere from $1,200 to $1,400 per month without hesitation. He also mentioned that this house would not be a great rental. It was in a higher-priced neighborhood, and the rents were pretty low based on the price of $189,900. The agent said they work with many investors, and most of them would never consider this as a rental. They want a good deal that would rent for much more compared to the price.

Mo was thinking that same thing, and it was great to hear someone else confirm his thoughts. He was beginning to think that real estate agents had no idea about investing. The agent asked the same questions as a couple of other agents had about talking to a lender and working with other agents. When Mo said he had not talked to a lender, the agent said he really needed to ASAP. The agent told him that for every investor that actually bought a house from him, there were ten more who wanted to be investors but would never even make an offer on an investment property.

That line discouraged Mo a little bit, but the agent told him he was not trying to scare him, just letting him know that if he really wanted to be an investor, he had to do more than look at houses, and the next step was talking to a lender.

Mo asked the agent about being able to rent out the house after he had lived there for a year, and that agent seemed to think that would be fine. Mo felt a wave of relief roll over him. His entire plan had not been shot down.

The agent gave Mo his card, which said his name was Ryan Wilson. Mo was sure the agent had told him his name before, but Mo had forgotten it. He was glad to get the card and the reminder.

"Well Ryan, do you have any lenders I can talk to?"

Ryan replied, "I sure do. I have a couple of lenders who I work with all the time, and they do a great job. You really must be careful because there is a big difference in lenders. Some are great, and some are horrible."

Mo gave Ryan his number and email address and told him that he would let him know what the lenders said. Ryan said he would send Mo more properties to consider once he had talked to the lender.

19

What is a good rental?

Mo spent the rest of the weekend going over the notes he had taken at each house. He brought his notebook with him and wrote down as much as he could about the properties, the agents, and any other information he could gather. None of the houses were close to working as rentals. The rents were too low and the prices too high. None of the houses were good deals either. He knew from his reading that a good deal was not easy to find. He would have to work hard to find those, and it most likely would not happen at open houses.

Mo decided to go over the numbers for fun on the last house he saw. He had learned that there are more expenses with rentals than just the property taxes, insurance, and mortgage. The house would need maintenance once in a while and it would not be rented all the time.

In the books, he had read most investors liked to calculate the possible expenses based on the rents. They may assume the maintenance costs for the house will be 10% of the monthly rents. If the house rents for $1,200 per month, the maintenance would be $120 per month. There would not be $120 of maintenance each month exactly. Some months there would be no maintenance and other months there could be hundreds or thousands of dollars in maintenance. The same went for vacancies.

Mo had also learned that the maintenance and vacancies varied on different types of properties. The older a property was, the more maintenance it would have. Different properties also had different costs associated with them.

Mo had liked single-family rentals from the start because he would be living in the house, and he wanted his own house. When he rented out the house, it was typical for the tenant to mow the lawn and pay all the utilities. On apartments, the landlord instead of the tenants usually mowed the lawn and took care of the place Plus, the landlord might pay for some of the utilities.

This is what he came up with on his first rental property analysis:

Purchase price: $189,900
  Rent amount: $1,300
  Taxes: $1,500
  Insurance: $800
  Maintenance: $108
  Vacancies: $54

Profit: -$1,162

A negative monthly profit! That was crazy. How could anyone make money with rental properties? Mo could not believe what he was coming up with. These numbers were not making much sense until Mo realized the insurance and taxes were for the year and the other expenses were monthly. So, he fixed his calculations and came up with his new numbers:

Rent: $1,300

Taxes: $125
Insurance: $66
Maintenance: $108
Vacancies: $54

Profit: $947 per month

That made more sense to Mo, although he was trying to figure out his numbers. From what he had read, the price-to-value ratio was not close to what he was looking for on this property. A lot of people said the rents should be 1% of the purchase price or higher. If the house was $189,900 like this one was, the rents should be at least $1,890 per month. This was actually a great rental property numbers wise, but Mo could not figure out why. Then he saw it.

He forgot to add the mortgage. If he paid cash for the property, it would make him about $950 per month. He went to an online mortgage calculator and punched in his numbers for a $189,000 mortgage. The mortgage would be over $1,050 per month! This property actually lost money every month as a rental with a loan.

It felt good to write the numbers down and see what a property would make. He knew in his gut that the house was not a good rental, but he had just confirmed it on his own! He wanted to find some houses that would make good rentals, and he thought about calling that last agent up, but he decided he needed to talk to a lender first. The agent was adamant that was his next step.

Mo was ready to take some more action. Today was a good day, and he was ready to keep moving forward.

20

Could he actually buy?

Mo called up one of the lenders that the last agent—what was his name...Ryan—had recommended to him. The lender's name was Josie, and she sounded like she knew what she was doing. They talked on the phone for a bit, and she asked Mo a few questions, but she really wanted to meet in person. Mo decided that he would meet Josie and see what she had to say. He was a little scared about what the lender would think of his finances, and he really just wanted to get this over with. He wanted her to tell him if he could buy a house or not over the phone, but he was realizing that was not going to happen.

He made an appointment to meet with Josie the next day. He figured the sooner he got this part of his learning curve over the better!

Mo met at Josie's office and was surprised at how easy going she was. It was not like the movies when the poor farmer goes to the bank to beg for a loan, and the banker in his expensive suit laughs him out of the building. Josie asked Mo about his job and the type of house he wanted and told Mo the basics of how a loan works. She wanted to pull Mo's credit, and he agreed but was worried that something was going to be terribly wrong. Mo was pretty careful about making his payments on time, but he knew once in a while he might be a little past the due date on his rent or other payments.

Josie must have been able to tell that Mo was nervous. She told him that even if there was a problem, they can usually get it fixed in a few months and get people's credit scores back to where they need to be.

The lender was able to get Mo's credit almost immediately, and he had a 670 score. Mo was not sure how good that was. He knew that something like an 800 was perfect, and most banks wanted to see scores in the 700s from what he had read. However, Josie told him his credit was great and he would have no problem getting a loan.

She went over the details about debt-to-income ratios, down payments, mortgage insurance, and many more things that Mo was somewhat familiar with but hadn't understood completely.

She said that Mo could get a 3.5% down payment loan with FHA or a 3% down payment loan with a conventional mortgage. If he went with FHA, he could qualify for a larger loan, but there would be more costs. The mortgage insurance was something that Mo was not expecting. Apparently, when you get a loan with less than 20% down, the banks charge mortgage insurance. That is insurance for the bank in case the borrower (Mo) goes into default. It was insurance that benefited the bank, and Mo was not sure why he was paying for that and not the bank, but he didn't think he had a chance of winning that argument.

Mo discovered that the mortgage insurance could add $100 to $200 per month to his mortgage payments, which really hurt the cash flow he was hoping to make when he eventually rented out the house. Mo was taking notes while the lender talked, and she mentioned something that was very interesting. If Mo were to get a conventional loan, he might be able to get the mortgage insurance removed when he had 20 or 25% equity in the house. Mo was planning to have that much equity almost immediately! The lender did say he had to wait at least 2 years with most loans to get the mortgage insurance removed, even if you walk into a house with instant equity.

Josie told Mo that besides the down payment, he would also have to come up with closing costs. The closing costs consisted of bank fees for the loan, closing company fees, the appraisal, and recording fees, and he learned he had to prepay for the insurance and property taxes when he bought the house. The closing costs were almost as much as the down payment.

She made a big deal about Mo not having to make a payment for two months after buying the house, but Mo knew that was not as amazing as it sounded from one of the articles he read online. That article mentioned you will not make a house payment the first month or two after buying a property, but that you still paid the interest during that time. In fact, you prepaid the interest when you got the loan. That prepaid interest is part of the closing costs. Josie mentioned that Mo may be able to get the seller to pay some of those closing costs to reduce the amount of money he needed at closing.

Part of Mo's plan was to buy a house that needed some work, and he mentioned that to Josie. She had more bad news for Mo. With most FHA and conventional loans, the house must be in a certain condition to get the loan. It cannot be in horrible shape or need a lot of repairs. There could be no peeling paint, holes in the walls, broken windows, or other major repairs.

That would limit the types of houses that Mo could buy, but honestly, he was not looking for a huge remodel job for his first house. Josie said there was nothing wrong with a dead yard, outdated homes, or properties that needed a little work. You could still get loans on them.

She told Mo that he could qualify for a house that cost around $200,000. She said that Mo was in pretty good shape. He had worked at his job for at least 2 years, had little debt, a small car payment, and decent credit. She mentioned that big car payments, credit card bills, and other debt can greatly limit the amount you can qualify for.

The last thing the lender did was print out and email Mo a pre-qualification letter. Mo felt pretty good when he saw that. He was officially able to buy a house if he found the right one and saved a little bit more money for the down payment and closing costs.

Mo felt wonderful walking out of Josie's office. He had been scared that something would pop up in his credit or on his finances that would stop the entire process. Now he knew he could buy a house—he could actually buy a house! He was thrilled, and he wanted to tell someone. However, he was not sure who to reach out to. He had pretty much stopped hanging out with Rob and Cory since they still only wanted to drink and drink a lot. He did not have any other real friends, and he was still getting to know the people at work. He decided he would be excited for himself for a while and tell some of the people at work on Monday during their relaxation time.

21

A challenge at work

Mo went to work that next Monday feeling great. He had not actually bought a house yet, and he knew when he did buy a house, he was still not an investor since he would be living in the house, but he felt great. One of the first things that happened at work that Monday was he got called into his boss's office. There goes that great feeling...

Here we go. Things were going great, and now here comes the bad news. He really did not know why Tory would want to talk to him. He was enjoying work. People were happy when he helped them, and he was even taking some initiative to help the company with improving their systems. Well, at least he was planning to help the company with their systems.

Mo walked into Tory's office, and Tory asked him to take a seat.

Tory started, "How are things going for you Mo? We don't really talk much, but you seem to be doing decent."

Mo replied, "Things are going well. I have a firm grasp on all the systems. There seem to be fewer issues coming up from the employees, and I am having more fun."

"I have noticed you are enjoying work more. A few of the staff have even mentioned your new demeanor to me. Honestly, I was a little bit worried about you there for a while. You couldn't get along with anyone, seemed miserable, and a few people complained that you were rude to them. Can I ask what changed?" Tory replied

Mo decided he should be honest with Tory. He told him, "I decided that even though this is not my dream job, it is a good job. While I may have higher aspirations for my life, I need to make the best of this while I am here and being pissed off all the time does not help anything or anyone."

Tory looked very surprised at Mo's answer. Mo was worried he may have been a little too honest. Tory thought for a second, relaxed a bit and told Mo, "Wow, that is a very honest answer, and I appreciate it. We are used to out tech people not having the best bedside manners, but we had high hopes for you when you were first hired. You seemed to have the smarts to do the job and a little more people skills than some of the other IT employees. I was pretty disappointed when things did not seem to be working out for you. In fact, I assumed you would be making your way up the corporate ladder by now."

Mo did not know how to respond to that. Tory was right, and Mo had expected more from himself as well. He started with, "You are right Tory, and I had higher expectations for myself. I am not sure what happened, but I got disenchanted along the way. It could be because I could do this work in my sleep, and I know I should be challenging myself."

Tory smiled at him and said, "I know you can do this work in your sleep, and so can most everyone else here. The thing is you have to prove to us you can do it and keep doing it with the right attitude before we can trust you with the heavier stuff. I think you have proven yourself the last couple of months, and I decided to give you a raise. We are going to up your salary to $45,000 per year. If you keep doing things right, those raises will keep coming, along with promotions."

Mo was happy. He did not think he would be so happy from a simple raise, but he was happy. He thanked Tory. They exchanged a few pleasantries, and he went back to his office. Mo realized he was happy not just because of the raise but because he was appreciated. There was a lot more to this job that he thought, and maybe there was a future for him here.

Mo realized that he should have expected some reward for doing a good job. If he was honest with himself, he did not do an amazing job in the past. He was negative, condescending to people, and was mostly waiting until his work day was over. No wonder he hated his job—he was putting nothing into it. When he started to perform a little better people noticed, including his bosses. Mo, was still not sure this was his dream job, but it felt good to be recognized.

When Mo's boss had mentioned a promotion, Mo thought he was talking about a manager position. Mo had always heard that managers did not make good money but were expected to work twice as hard. Mo was thinking about who always told him being a manager was not all it was cracked up to be. It was the guys in the mail room who had no ambition and mostly just wanted to make enough money to buy weed.

Mo had realized something when he was doing all of his real estate research: you have to be very careful who you listen to, and you cannot take someone's word for something. If you hear something that sounds exciting, crazy, or just interesting, verify it. People love to tell stories, so that can get some attention...whether they are true or not. Other people repeat those stories, and eventually it becomes a fact, a bit like the rumor that there is a shortage of cork in the world, and that is why wine companies started to make twist off caps. The truth is there is plenty of cork in the world—the wine companies are just saving money.

Mo decided he needed to look into what managers actually made at his company before he discounted the position. He started to ask some of the co-workers who he had gotten to know a little better. Most of them were not managers, but a few were. He felt comfortable talking to them now, and what was the worst that could happen if he started asking them about the management positions and how much money they made? They could not tell him. It was not like they would report him to his superiors for asking about being a manager.

Mo wanted to ask Sarah about the manager position. She was not a manager but seemed to do her job well and kept in the loop with the company. He decided he did not want to talk about the subject in front of everyone else at the office, so he asked her if she had plans for lunch. This was a big step for Mo. He convinced himself he was only asking her to lunch because he wanted to learn about the management position, but deep down he knew he also wanted to get to know Sarah a little better. With his new attitude about work and life he saw that she was actually pretty smart. Most likely, she had no problem working her email but wanted an excuse to talk to him. When he asked her to lunch, she thought about it for a second or two and then agreed.

Mo had forgotten about the weekend and learning he could qualify for a house! He had a lot to talk about!

22

Who wants lunch?

Mo walked over to Sarah's desk a little before noon, and she was on the phone. She signaled with her finger for him to wait a second while she finished up her call. She hung up a second later and asked Mo if he was ready to go.

"I wouldn't be standing here if I wasn't," He joked. Mo could be a bit of a smart ass.

Sarah didn't seem to care and replied, "Well let's get some food, I am starving! I know a great little sandwich place not too far away."

They walked out of the office and down the street to a sandwich place a block from work. They chatted about work and other things on the walk over. Mo had a few things he wanted to bring up but wanted to wait until they got settled in for lunch.

They arrived at the little shop, which Mo had been to before. He loved a good club sandwich, and they had plenty of those. They ordered, and Mo insisted on paying for both of them. He said told Sarah that he had invited her to lunch, so he was supposed to pay for it. Plus, he wanted to get some super-important information out of her.

They sat down at a table that was outside on a little patio overlooking the street.

Mo started right in, "Thanks for meeting with me. I have a few things I wanted to get your opinion on."

"No problem", she said

Mo said, "I have worked at the company for a while and really never took his job seriously. I recently decided to make some huge changes in my life, and one of the changes was being less negative and embracing this job."

She replied, "I noticed! I think it is a welcome change, and other people have noticed as well. I don't think anyone ever saw you smile until a month ago."

Mo continued, "It is a little more fun not being mad at everything. I can tell you that. I also feel a lot more productive and realized my job is not as horrible as I have always thought it was."

"I can see why you are not thrilled with your job. It is not the most exciting work environment," she said

"True. It is not exactly what I envisioned myself doing when I was younger," Mo replied.

Sarah said, " What exactly did you envision when you were younger?"

Mo thought for a second. He had not really considered what he really wanted to do in life or what he had pictured himself doing for a long time.

He said, "That is a really good question. I guess I don't think about what I want very often, just what I don't want, at least with work. I think when I was younger, I thought I would be a genius computer hacker or programmer or something."

Sarah asked, "What happened to that dream? When did you stop believing in it?"

Mo paused again then said, "I think in college I stopped believing in it. They teach you how to get a job in college. They teach you skills that will get you hired at a place like this. They don't really teach you how to be a hacker or do what you love."

Mo realized this conversation was not going where he wanted it to go. He wanted to talk about his real estate ventures and his promotion. Why were they talking about his long lost dreams? He decided to turn the tables a little.

"What about your dreams? Did you envision working in a place like this?"

Sarah said, "Maybe. I always wanted to be an accountant. I like numbers and order and figured most accountants work in a place like this or somewhere doing taxes. I am by no means satisfied with my position,but I have been working my way up, and I always keep my eyes open for better opportunities. You are right—I could be more more ambitious, but I am also pretty happy with simple things. I can tell you were not happy with work, but you didn't really do anything to change it until recently."

"Good point, but anyway, that brings up one reason I wanted to talk to you. I got a raise the other day, and Tory told me if I kept it up, I would get a manager position."

Sarah exclaimed, "That's great! Congrats!"

"That is one thing I wanted to talk to you about. A lot of my friends, well...old friends, they weren't even friends if I am being honest, anyway. They said being a manager sucks. It is more work, more hours, more hassles, and not that much more money."

Sarah thought for a second about what he said, then responded, "First, I think you have to consider where this information came from. I don't think those guys you talked to have the biggest dreams in the world, to put it nicely. However, there is some truth to that. There is more work. There may be longer hours, and the pay increase may not be worth it to some people. However, to other people, it may be more than worth it. If you have that manager position on your resume, it will help immensely if you ever want another job or get laid off or something. You also get to learn much more about the inner workings of the company—why and how they do things. This may not seem like an exciting place to you, but they are very successful and know how to run a business. Lastly, you will be networking and meeting with much more important people. You never know how they could help you in the future."

Mo sat there for a bit contemplating what she said. He had not thought of many of these things. He was mostly thinking about the money versus the work and time it would take to be a manager. He decided right then that being a manager would be worth it, even if he got the same pay. He still had to ask:

"Do you know how much they make?"

Sarah smiled and said, "One million dollars!"

She chuckled and continued, "I am not really sure as it varies based on the department, experience, etc. I have talked to a few people and inquired for myself. I would say from $60,000 to $100,000."

"Oh!" Mo was not expecting that. It was not a million dollars, but that was a really decent salary, especially with the benefits they got at the company.

"That settles that. I will take the manager position assuming they ever offer it!"

Mo had a lot spinning around in his head. They had talked about many things and eaten their food. He realized they needed to head back to work soon. He mentioned they should get going and Sarah agreed. They started to walk back to the office.

"There was something else I wanted to tell you," he said.

"What's that?" she said as she looked up at him.

"You remember how I said I was trying to buy a house a while back? Well I have been working really hard to find something. I looked at some houses this weekend. I did not find any I liked, but I found a cool agent, and I talked to a lender. She said I could qualify for a loan!"

"That is awesome," she said matter of factually, "I knew you could do it"

Sarah seemed to be genuinely excited about Mo's plans for real estate. Mo felt amazing, not because Sarah was confident in him, well maybe a little because of that, but mostly because this was the first person who had been encouraging about his real estate endeavor. That was not entirely true, some of the guys that he hung with on Mondays from work had not thought it was a good idea to invest in real estate, but they could have just been being polite.

Mo knew he was on the right track with more than a few things in his life. It seemed pretty simple now, but a year or two ago he would have made fun of himself for trying at work and not going out all the time with his friends.

He had a long way to go, but things were looking up, and he had a lot to look forward to. Speaking of the guys he hung out with after work, he decided to skip the Monday relaxing dinner. He wanted to focus on his real estate, and telling Sarah what he was thinking seemed to satisfy his need to tell someone about his amazing weekend.

23

Taking care of those who help

Something else that Mo had learned during his "learning phase" was that good real estate agents were hard to find. It felt really good calling his last phase the learning phase because that meant that he was in the next phase, which he dubbed the "action phase."

A lot of his research led him to believe that when you found a really good real estate agent, you did whatever you could to keep that agent on your side. Mo was not sure exactly how to do that, but he had a simple idea. He would buy Ryan lunch. Mo did not have a lot of money, and he knew that Ryan had a lot more money than him, but supposedly making a simple gesture like buying lunch could help get him on his agent's good side.

Mo called Ryan and told him the good news first. He had talked to Josie and gotten pre-qualified! He was now one step closer to buying a house. He asked Ryan if he could take him to lunch some time to go over what his plans were. Ryan seemed a bit surprised but agreed, and they set up a time and place two days later.

Mo wanted to be prepared for his lunch meeting with Ryan. He wanted to be prepared for everything now. He was tired of just showing up and hoping things worked out for him. Mo wrote out the bullet points of his plan. He wanted to go over everything with Ryan and see what his thoughts were. Mo was not dead set on doing whatever Ryan thought was best, but he wanted to hear his opinion. Ryan had money, seemed to know what he was talking about, and could be an amazing resource.

The day for lunch arrived, and Mo was excited. He left work a little earlier than he was supposed to for lunch, but no one noticed and probably would not care even if they did notice. He got to the restaurant 10 minutes early. Normally, he would have waited in his car until he saw whoever he was meeting get to the restaurant. He would not want to look like an idiot sitting at a table waiting by himself. But today, Mo walked right in and got a table for him and Ryan. He was too worked up to worry about what other people thought of him today. He sent Ryan a text saying he arrived a little early and got them a table.

A light ping of doubt entered Mo's mind as he thought about Ryan not showing and himself sitting there all alone waiting and waiting and waiting. Then, Ryan texted back and said he would be there in a few minutes. Mo laughed and wondered how those crazy thoughts enter our minds. Maybe if he was on a date, it would make more sense!

Ryan showed up in a few minutes and sat across from Mo.

He said, "How is it going? Good to see you again!"

Mo replied, "I am great. Thanks for having lunch with me. I know your time is valuable, and I appreciate it."

Ryan said, "No worries at all. I was a little surprised when you said you wanted to buy me lunch. Most of my clients expect me to buy them lunch or coffee since I am earning a commission when they buy or sell a house."

Mo decided to be straight up with Ryan. He said, "Well, I am a real estate investor. I mean, I want to be a real estate investor. That is, I will be a real estate investor! I have done a lot of research, and I know that most people who want to be investors never buy anything. I wanted to make sure you knew I was serious. That is also why I made sure I got pre-qualified so quickly."

Ryan replied, "Yes, that was a good move. A lot of people will put that off and assume I will keep showing them houses. You getting that done so fast let me know that you are serious. And, the lunch helps!"

The waiter came by to take their order, but since they had been talking, they both had no idea what they wanted to eat. They asked for a few more minutes to decide and stared at their menus in silence. The waiter came back. They ordered, and Mo got right back into his pitch.

He told Ryan, "I will be honest with you—I do not have a lot of money. I wish I had the 20% down for a rental, but I don't. I have some money, and my plan is to buy a house as an owner occupant so I can get the lower down payment, live there a year, and then turn it into a rental."

Ryan said, "Yes, I remember you mentioning that before. That is not a bad idea. You can buy a house much cheaper when you live in it, and you are young and free!'

Mo smiled and continued, "Something I wanted to ask you was about buying a house in general. I was never taught much about investing or real estate. I always thought buying a house was what you were supposed to do, but I read *Rich Dad Poor Dad,* and he talks about how bad it is to buy a house to live in. It sort of made sense to me, but now that I had learned about buying as an owner occupant and then renting out the property, I am confused. I wanted to make sure I was not missing something."

Ryan smiled and said, "First off, you are asking a guy who sells houses if buying houses is a good idea. So obviously, my answer is *Rich Dad Poor Dad* is a horrible book, and you should not listen to anything said in it!" Ryan laughed and kept talking, "Mo, I am just joking around. *Rich Dad Poor Dad* is a great book, but it is not the end all be all for financial freedom. It is very motivational and has some great concepts but has some things in it I disagree on as well."

Mo Said, "That is what I thought too, but I would love to hear why you think that."

Ryan replied, "Fair enough. You bought me lunch, so I will keep talking. *Rich Dad Poor Dad* and even guys like Grant Cardone say buying a house to live in is bad. However. there are many things you must consider when they say this.

"First, they are both marketers, and the more outrageous or contrarian their claims are, the more they get in the news, and the more money they make. They specialize in selling coaching, not buying real estate. They have millions and millions of dollars to invest. They don't have the same mindset as the average Joe trying to squeeze every penny as far as it can go. For most of the population, the only option to buy a house is to own it as an owner occupant. They both preach that real estate is amazing, but if you can't buy it using their techniques what good is it?

Second, most people's net worth is from their home. You can talk about how bad an investment a home is, but the facts say that if someone is middle aged, almost 70% of their net worth is from their home. It is a forced savings plan for most people. If you are a savvy investor, you can make even greater gains with a personal house. Those guys don't mention that the profit on a home you live in is almost always tax free if you live there for at least 2 years. Not tax deferred, but tax free. You can also get a great deal on a house, which means you walk into the deal with tens of thousands of dollars in equity. You can get the best loans on an owner-occupied house with the least amount of money down. If you have equity in the house you live in, they are the easiest to refinance or get a line of credit on. Some sellers like HUD or banks will give owner occupants the first chance to buy a house over investors.

Finally, you have to pay rent if you don't own. In many places, the rent is higher than the mortgage payment on a house. While a house might cost you money to live in, I know a rental will cost you money to live in and you won't have a thing to show for it. When you own, you also do not have to worry about being kicked out of the place when the landlord decides to sell or the rents being raised every year."

Mo looked at Ryan in awe, "Wow! You really had that speech ready to go didn't you?"

Ryan replied, "Yes. You could say I have given it a few times. The facts are, I have seen many people make a lot of money with investment properties and with their own personal house. To me, real estate is an amazing tool to amass wealth with not that much risk involved."

Mo wanted to learn as much as he could and had one last question, "I can see real estate is great when the market goes up, but what if things crash like they did ten years ago?"

Ryan appeared to be ready for this one as well, "That is an awesome question. Real estate does not always go up. In fact, it can go down, and the last crash hurt a lot of people. Another fact many people do not know is about 8% of investor loans went into foreclosure that were taken out right before the crash. You had the worst loans being given at a time when prices were artificially high because bad loans were pushing prices up, and only 8% of those loans went into foreclosure.

Now, to be fair, there could have been some short sales going on when a bank allows the investor to sell for a loss. But the idea that every investor went bankrupt in the last crash is not true. For homeowners, it is even better."

Mo asked, "Better?"

Ryan said, "Better...because they live in the home. When someone lives in a home, the bank cannot simply kick them out as soon as they are behind on payments. The bank has to go through the foreclosure process, which can take months or years in some states. Guess what? That entire time, the homeowners can live in the home. Is it better to get evicted from a rental in a month or two or to live in your house rent free for months or years?"

Mo could not say anything but, "Be a homeowner."

Ryan replied, "Right. On top of the rent-free arrangement the bank cannot avoid, they will offer cash for keys, which means they will pay the homeowner thousands of dollars to move out peacefully so they can avoid an eviction. They may even offer money to the homeowner to sell the house as a short sale. They could offer a loan modification, which means the payments and principal of the loan are reduced to help the homeowner stay afloat."

Mo responded, "Wow. So basically, the homeowner can work the system to stay rent free for months or years and then get paid to move out?"

Ryan said, "Yup! The downside to owning a house is not as bad as many people make it out to be."

Mo said, "Ryan, you know you are really good at your job right?"

Ryan smiled and said, "Yes, and I love every second of it. One more thing to add after all of that. *Rich Dad Poor Dad* actually does not say it is stupid to buy a house to live in. It says you should not spend all your money on the house you live in. Too many people become 'house poor' by spending as much as they possibly can."

Mo was convinced more than ever that he had the right agent on his side. He also saw the advantages of buying a house as a homeowner and was ready to move forward. Buying Ryan lunch was the best investment he had ever made.

24

Finding the right people

Mo had a decent job with a possible promotion! He had a pre-qualification letter from the bank. He had a great real estate agent who had been sending him houses that were for sale. He was excited about his life and where things could go. He knew he could not take things easy and hope everything worked out. He had to make it happen if he really wanted to succeed at this real estate thing.

Since their lunch, Ryan had sent Mo quite a few house listings. Just about all of them were better possibilities than the open house Mo attended. That was not hard to do, but it was still promising that maybe Mo had found an agent who understood what Mo wanted. Mo knew now for sure that he had to buy a house to live in first. Then, he could turn that house into a rental eventually. That was the fastest possible way for him to get his first rental.

Mo did not feel like any of the houses Ryan sent him were the "right" property, but he knew he was on the right track. The properties needed a little bit of work and had much better price-to-rent ratios. Mo knew he needed to see some of these houses in order to get a better feel for the market and what he wanted. He wanted a house that he could live in but fix up at the same time. It could not be too dilapidated, needed

to be somewhat close to work, and he had to be able to r[...]
he was ready to move on.

Ryan had been adamant that Mo get his pre-qualificatio[...]
he showed him more houses. Since Mo was able to get the letter, Ryan
was much more willing to help him.

One thing Mo had read was agents can often be wary working with
investors because so many people who want to invest in real estate
rarely ever buy an investment property. Real estate agents only get
paid when they sell a house. They earn a commission by either working
with the buyer or the seller. If they work 100 hours with a buyer who
never purchases a home, they have basically worked those 100 hours
for free. The really good agents make sure the buyers they work with
are serious and are taking action to buy a property. Mo wanted Ryan
to think he was serious. That was one reason he took him to lunch.

Mo also learned that there are good real estate agents and bad real
estate agents. There tend to be many more bad agents than good. It is
imperative that a real estate investor finds the right agent for them
and shows that agent that they are serious about buying a property.

Mo had also read on one of the blogs that it is also not the real estate
agent's job to invest for the investors. The investor should know what
kind of property they want, where they want it, and what the numbers
should look like. After all, every investor and person is different in
what type of property they are looking for. The agent's job is to find
what the buyer wants, not decide what the buyer wants. Mo may have
gotten very lucky finding Ryan, who seemed to be responsive with
plenty of investment knowledge.

Mo was doing everything he could to show Ryan that he was serious
and that he knew what he was doing. Mo had been encouraged by the

..er agents he met at open houses. He felt like he knew more about investing than they did. With that confidence he no longer felt like he was pretending to know what he was doing and that at any point he would be "found out."

Ryan seemed to be the perfect agent. He knew about investing, and he was competent. Mo was still not going to let Ryan make all the decisions or decide what he should buy. That was Mo's job, and he had worked hard to educate himself on the best way to buy an investment property.

Now, it was time to see some more properties and get serious about finding the right house.

25

Jump in with both feet

Mo met the Ryan at the first of 5 houses they were set to see on a Saturday. He was beginning to wonder how real estate agents did it. They only made money when a house sold. They had to work all the time, including the weekends, and they could put hours upon hours in with one client who may never buy a home.

When Ryan showed up, he was driving a fairly new Audi S8—a $120,000 car. Mo thought *I guess being an agent is not that bad*!

Ryan jumped out of the car and asked Mo how he was doing. At the same time, he handed Mo a stack of papers. Ryan said, "These are MLS sheets. That stands for multiple listing service."

Mo replied, "I know what MLS stands for. I have been doing my research"

"Alright, alright. I never know how much a new client knows about how all this works." Ryan said. He was smiling when he said it, and Mo knew he had a good sense of humor and was a pretty laid back guy.

Ryan continued, "These are MLS sheets for the houses I have set up for today. I don't know if any of these will work for you, but a lot of my investors can take months before they find the right deal. Don't get frustrated if we don't find something right away. The best investment properties are not just sitting out there waiting to be bought. It takes some work to get them."

I only have a couple of hours free, so we can't spend an hour at each house. I am happy to work with investors, but they need to respect my time. I am not here to be a coach, but I will help if I can."

"I got you," Mo said, trying to act cool.

Ryan had arranged the sheets so they were in the order of the house viewings. Mo quickly glanced at all the sheets and then focused on the first one—the house they were standing in front of.

The house was listed at $120,000, which was a great price point for Mo. I looked a little rough on the outside, but that was no problem for Mo.

"We started with one of the worst homes first. I work as efficiently as possible, and I figured you could handle it," Ryan said as they walked up the sidewalk to the front door. Ryan rang the doorbell and knocked before he entered a code into a box and retrieved the key. He knocked again and said hello as he unlocked the door.

"I think this one would rent out for $1,400 per month with some repairs," Ryan said

Mo followed Ryan through the front door and was hit with a smell he had never experienced before. It was a mix of mold, dirt, and dead animals. It was not pleasant, and Mo could not help blurt, "Oh man, that is bad!"

Ryan looked at him and said, "I thought you were serious about this."

Ryan did not seem to be bothered by the smell, nor did he seem to be joking, so Mo sucked it up. They entered the house in the living room, and Mo could see why Ryan said it was in bad shape. There was carpet, but he could not tell what color it used to be. Now it was a brownish black with what looked like used motor oil rubbed into it. In a few spots, the carpet was worn all the way through to the wood below it. There was no hardwood under these floors, just plywood.

Ryan did not say a word, and he let Mo walk through the house. Mo could tell Ryan was watching him and his reactions. He felt like this was a test to see if he would be worth Ryan's time or not. He didn't complain about how awful the house was or pretend to know how much the repairs would cost. Mo kept quiet as well and started making notes on his notebook he had brought with him. He had his phone too.

"Can I take pictures?" Mo asked.

"Sure. This house is vacant and it is fine to take a few pictures."

Mo walked through the house and was not impressed at all. Through the living room was the dining room, which also had worn-out carpet. There was a sliding glass door to the backyard that was boarded up because the glass had shattered. He then entered the kitchen, which was beside the dining room and behind the living room. There was a wall between the living room and the kitchen. It was definitely not an open floor plan that was always talked about on TV.

The kitchen was a mess. The cabinets were about 40 years old and falling apart. They were flimsy particle board, and a few doors had holes in them or were missing. The drawers were falling out, and there was not even a spot for the dishwasher. The floor was old vinyl with

95

holes in it showing the plywood underneath.

The rest of the house was the same. There were broken windows, baths were horrible, the basement was a dungeon, and Mo did not want to spend anymore time down there than he had to. After seeing most of the house, he turned to Ryan, "I know you said this house needed a lot of work, but this is bad. I don't think I could ever get a loan on it, even if I was willing to take all of this on."

Ryan said, "I wanted to show you a wide range of houses. This is the worst we will see. I have also not seen this house before, and I was not sure how bad it was until I peaked into it a little before you got here. You never know how good or bad a house is until you see it. The pictures can make a house look much worse or better than it actually is."

"I guess that makes sense," Mo said as he looked at the MLS sheet. The outside picture they used did not look bad at all. The description said the home needed some TLC but was not very honest about how bad the house was.

Mo continued, "This MLS sheet is almost lying. This house is way worse that it say sit is. Are they allowed to do that?"

Ryan replied, "Yes. They are representing the seller. If they made the house sound horrible, they would not be doing a good job for their client. They aren't lying about anything, just leaving a few things out."

Mo thought for a second then said, "So what you are saying is that we need to look at a lot of houses because you can't always tell from the MLS what is a good or bad deal?"

"Exactly. That is also why I make sure I vet each buyer I work with. It can take a lot of time on my side to show these houses. I don't want to show 50 houses and then learn you don't really want to buy a house or can't qualify for a loan."

Mo realized they were still in the house and he had gotten used to the smell. Well, now that he thought about it he noticed it again. He knew there would be a few things he had to get used to if he wanted to be an investor.

Ryan started to talk again, "Besides, you probably could buy this house if you really wanted to. I am not saying you should, but there are loans that help with the repairs."

Ryan told Mo about the FHA 203k rehab loan. Mo could buy a house that needs a ton of work with that loan and finance most of the repairs.

Mo was intrigued but knew this was a huge project. He was also wondering why the lender he had talked to had never mentioned the 203K FHA loan to him. Ryan said that most lenders do not want to do the 203k loans or are not qualified to do them. They can take a long time to complete, are more expensive, and you have to jump through many hoops to make them work. He also said that you must have an approved 203k contractor do most of the work on the home, which can be very expensive.

Mo was starting to wonder how much more complicated real estate could become.

Mo looked at the other houses Ryan had set up for them. They went through the them pretty quickly, but Mo was beginning to learn what to look for without spending an hour at each property. Ryan was also helping Mo figure out what a home would be worth after a little work was done to it. Mo didn't want to buy a house for $120,000, spend

$20,000 fixing it up, and have the home be worth $140,000. He didn't even want that house to be worth $150,000. He wanted to buy a house for $120,000, spend $20,000 fixing it up (or less if possible), and have it be worth $170,000 or more when he was done. In a perfect world, he would spend $5,000 fixing up the house because he didn't actually have the $20,000 to spend on the repairs. He figured with his own sweat equity, he could save a lot of money on the work. Although, he didn't really have any idea how to actually complete the repairs.

The other houses were decent, but none of them jumped out at him. Mo wanted to make sure he found the right house to start off with and did not jump into something too quickly.

Mo was leaving the last house when he told Ryan, "Thanks for showing me all these. I really appreciate it. It opened my eyes to what is available and how much work some of these will need. I don't think we found the house yet, but I am getting a better idea of what I want."

Ryan said, "No problem. This is just the beginning, and it's my job to help you through all of this."

Ryan pointed at Mo's notebook, "Run the numbers on these and see if any of them make money. Even if you don't want to buy them, it's great practice."

They said goodbye, and Mo headed home.

26

Can I afford this?

O n the way home, Mo decided he really needed to look at his finances since he was closer than ever to finding a house. He knew he had to have some down payment money, and he knew he might need some money for closing costs as well. The lender had given him a rough idea of the money he would need, but he had not sat down and written everything out.

He figured he would buy a house in the $100,000 to $150,000 price range. The costs would vary quite a bit depending on how much he spent. He assumed the down payment would be 3% with the conventional loan he was going to get. That would mean he could spend $3,000 on a $100,000 house or $4,500 on a $150,000 house.

The lender also said that the closing costs would be about 2 to 3% of the loan. That would be another $2,000 to $4,500 on top of the down payment. Mo had been saving money from work, but he had not saved that much money. He had saved about $3,000. Now he knew he really had to be patient because he did not quite have the money to buy a house yet.

Mo had remembered something about the closing costs being paid for the buyer in some cases. He sent Ryan a text and asked him how that worked. Ryan replied a few minutes later and said that some sellers were willing to raise the price of the house in order to pay for the buyer closing costs. If the house was $100,000, but the buyer wanted the seller to pay for their closing costs, the price would have to be $103,000 for the offer to be the same as a $100,000 offer with no closing costs.

Mo thanked him with another text.

If the seller paid for Mo's closing costs, it would save him cash, but he would have to pay more for the house. He decided that since he was so short on cash at the moment, he would gladly pay a little more for the house and have his closing costs paid for.

Mo also decided he wanted to stay on the low end of his price range to save money. He had enough money right now to barely buy a house, but he thought it was smart to save a little more before he purchased something.

Mo also did what Ryan told him to do. He ran some of the numbers on the houses they looked at. He had a rough idea of what the houses would rent for. He knew how to use an online mortgage calculator to calculate his mortgage payment. He could see the property taxes on the MLS sheets. He knew roughly what the insurance would be. He was also sure to add on the maintenance and vacancy costs.

These houses were much better rentals than the first houses he saw on his own. The big unknown was the repair costs. Most of the houses that Ryan showed him needed a lot of work. Mo could do some of it but not all of it. He was not sure how much a remodel would cost. He could ask Ryan, but he figured he had taken enough of his time for the day.

Mo was not sure if he was happy to see the houses and make progress or stressed because it felt like there was so much more to do and learn. He went with happy.

27

How do you actually buy a house?

After talking to Ryan, Mo was also learning more about how the house-buying process worked. There were a lot of moving parts, and he realized he knew absolutely nothing when he started this process. Not only did he have to learn about the investing side, but he also had to learn about how to actually buy that investment property.

Mo met with Ryan a few more times and learned more every time.

The buying process starts with an offer. The real estate agent writes the offer on a state-approved form. The offer includes the purchase price, loan information, closing date, inspection contingency date, appraisal date, loan conditions date, what is included with the property, and a few other items.

Ryan was very helpful in explaining how it all worked. He mentioned that every real estate deal is a little different, and every state does things a little differently. Some states use title companies while others use attorneys. It can be customary for the seller to pay for some costs in one area, but the buyer may pay those costs in another area. The agent said that is one reason why it is so important for buyers and sellers to use real estate agents.

The inspection was something everyone recommended he get. A home inspection is when a home inspector checks a house to see what problems it may have. The inspector will check out the furnace, air conditioning, roof, electrical system, plumbing, appliances, foundation, and most things visible in the home. Now, the home inspector is not an expert in every single aspect of a home. However, the inspector can usually point out problems that can be evaluated fully by a licensed professional.

In most states, when you get a home inspection, you are allowed a certain amount of time to conduct it and ask the seller to fix any problems. You can also ask the seller to give a credit or even cancel your contract based on the inspection. You also get your earnest money back if you cancel your inspection or you cancel the contract in the allotted amount of time given in the contract.

Ryan explained how some real estate investors will use the home inspection as a way to negotiate more with the seller. Ryan told him that the best option is to use the home inspection for real issues that might be deal killers. If Mo wants to be a serious real state investor in this town, he needs to start building a good reputation right now. His agent said that many investors try to nickel and dime everybody in every instance they can. Ryan told Mo that he had worked with an investor who created so many bad feelings on the deals they did that agents stopped working with them. He said after a while other agents thought it was Ryan who was always trying to negotiate every single thing. Ryan dropped the investor to protect his reputation since the investor refused to change their ways.

Mo also learned how earnest money works. When you write the contract, you put in the contract the amount of earnest money you are going to pay. The amount is usually close to 1% of the purchase price. If the contract is accepted, the buyer must pay that earnest money to the tile company or attorney depending on which state you live in. The title company will hold that earnest money until the property closes or the contract falls apart. The contract will dictate whether the seller or the buyer gets the earnest money back if the contract fails. In some states, it's very hard to lose your earnest money unless you get to the day before closing and then decide to cancel your contract. In other states, it can be a little easier to lose your earnest money, and you have to be very careful about your dates and what properties you offer on. The earnest money is applied towards the purchase of the home as part of your down payment.

Mo also learned the title company that handles the closing makes sure there are no liens against the property and provides title insurance. If you're going to get a loan on a house, you need title insurance so the bank knows there are no other loans or liens against the property. The title company provides all these services, and most of the fees are customarily paid by the seller. It also customary that the seller picks a title company since they are paying most of those fees.

When getting a loan on a property, the buyer will also need an appraisal. The appraisal is ordered by the buyer's lender and is used to determine the value of the property. The appraisal will tell the bank if the property is worth what the contract price says the buyer is willing to pay. If the appraisal comes in lower than the contract price, the buyer's loan is based on that lower appraised value not the contract price. So many times, lower appraisals can cause issues with properties because a buyer must bring more cash or the seller must lower the price of the property in order for the buyer to purchase it. Usually, the buyer pays for the appraisal as part of their closing cost. And if the buyer orders and appraisal and the home does not close, the buyer could be stuck paying that cost, which could be from $400 to $800 depending on the area and the size of the home.

It was tough for Mo to remember all of this, but he had learned some of it in the books and articles he read. The more he became immersed in this process, the more he remembered. He also had Ryan, who could remind him how everything worked.

Ryan was also quick to remind Mo that most buyers never fully understand the process of buying or selling a house. They depend on their agent or lender to do everything for them. Many times, the buyers and sellers do just fine letting the agents or lenders handle everything, but the more a client knows, the better off they will be. Ryan told Mo it was actually nice to have a buyer who cared so much and wanted to learn all the details on how the process worked.

Mo was beginning to wonder if he was better off learning all of this...or if it would give him just enough knowledge to be dangerous.

28

The promotion

A couple of weeks went by with Mo continuing to work hard to save his money. He was also hoping the perfect house would come on the market. He knew he didn't need the perfect house, but he wanted a property that would be right for him. It had to be a good deal, rent out for enough compared to the purchase price, and be in the right price range.

He was at work one morning when Tory called him into his office. Mo no longer worried that he might get fired or get yelled at for slacking off at work.

Today, Mo was excited because it was probably a good thing he was being called into his boss's office. He headed over to the office, knocked on the door, and Tory told him to come in and have a seat.

After Mo sat down, Tory started in, "How has everything been going at work?"

Mo replied, "Great! I feel like I am making strides towards helping out more, and I have a better attitude about things."

Tory said, "I noticed you have had a great attitude. I was worried that your new attitude we talked about before may be short lived. A lot of people show short-term improvements but then go back to their old habits."

Mo said, "Thank you. I will be honest with you and say I still do not know if this is my dream job, but it is a lot more enjoyable when I have a better attitude."

"I think you are ready for that promotion," Tory said.

Mo smiled and said, "I figured that was what this meeting was about. I did not want to get my hopes up, just in case you had other plans."

Tory said, "No, you have been a great asset in the office, and we want to make sure you stick around. I think a more-challenging position make make work even more enjoyable for you. I am going to make you a manager, but I know you have zero experience being a manager. We will start you out slowly and guide you along the way. I don't want you to freak out thinking you are in over your head. The first thing we are going to do is make you the head of that little office you occupy with the other IT staff. We don't have a manager in that position right now, and we mostly let you guys do whatever you want."

Mo thanked Tory and went back to his office. He was not sure how excited he was to be managing his "little office," but it was better than not managing anyone. It would not be difficult to tell the other guys what to do as they were competent and fairly decent at their jobs.

Mo had not brought up his ideas for improving things yet. He had been preoccupied with real estate and was not sure if he wanted to rock the boat when things had been going so well at work. Now that he had a management position, it might be a great opportunity to put some kind of proposal together for improving the IT systems in the office.

Mo decided to find Sarah so he could tell her about the good news. He was beginning to think that he and Sarah might have something. The only problem is they work together, which is frowned upon. Again, in the past, Mo would not have cared about them working together because he did not care about his job that much. But now that he got a promotion and he enjoyed his work, he was a little worried about losing his job, especially because that would make buying a house very difficult.

Something Mo had learned from the lender was how important it was to have a solid job when buying a house. Most lenders want to see someone work at the same job for at least 2 years...or at least work in the same line of work for at least 2 years. The lender wants to see stability in the person's job so they know they will continue to work there and will be able to make their payments.

If Mo were to lose his job, it would make it very tough for him to qualify for a loan and to buy his first house. That made things a little tough between him and Sarah if they ever did start to date because Mo did not want to waste all the knowledge and experience he had gained in the real estate business.

Honestly, Mo did not know the exact policy at work about dating coworkers. However, he figured there was something in all the paperwork he signed when he took the job. Over the last few months, Mo had learned it was not safe to assume anything. He should check out the policy eventually if things progressed any further with Sarah. For right now, they were strictly friends.

He found her at her desk working away like usual. She appeared to be a very hard worker. She was not standing around gossiping in the break room like many of the other employees. She was not browsing all kinds of personal websites during work either, like most people did.

Mo could see all of that since that was his specialty.

He maneuvered himself in front of her desk so she could see he was standing there. She looked up, and he said, "Hi."

"What's going on?" she replied

"I just got out of a meeting with Tory, and I got the manager position!"

"That is awesome. Hard work pays off," Sarah replied, but Mo could tell her heart was not in it. He thought she would be excited for him, but he could tell there was some hesitation. He was not one to delve too deep into people's emotions or thoughts, especially at work. He decided to leave it alone for now. He was thinking about asking her to lunch, but he decided that was not the best idea today.

He felt a little weird after their short conversation. He could tell she did not want to talk very much, so he went back to his office. He was not going to let that get him down. He had gotten a promotion, and he was proud of it!

29

Act fast!

L ater that afternoon, while Mo was getting ready to leave the office, Ryan texted him. He said a house just popped up for sale that they needed to see. Mo was able to search for houses online, but Ryan always seemed to find them faster. He supposed that was because it was Ryan's job.

Ryan told Mo to meet him at the house after work because he thought this house would sell fast. Mo agreed and said he'd head straight over once he left the office.

Mo pulled up to the house and saw Ryan's S8 already in front. There was no real estate sign yet, and it appeared there were other people already looking at the home. There was a car in the driveway, and the front door was open.

Mo got out of his car and greeted Ryan, "Thanks for telling me about this. Nice car by the way. I have been meaning to tell you that for a while."

Ryan replied, "Thanks! I love cars, and I am fortunate that real estate has allowed me to buy a machine like this. A 600 horsepower twin turbo V8 isn't too shabby either."

Mo said, "It is a sweet car. One day I would like to get something just a little nicer than my 5-year-old Maxima, but anyway, I wanted to ask you something. How did you find out about this listing so fast? I am always checking and have a search notification set up with Zillow for new listings."

Ryan said, "Zillow can be a great resource, but they are a little slow with new listings. My MLS access is much faster, and the search notifications I get are instant."

Mo replied, "That is not fair you get to see stuff before me. What's up with that?"

"Well, you have to remember that real estate agents created and supply the MLS and Zillow with listings. Zillow just copies what the agents enter. It only makes sense that agents get some advantage since they do all the work. Some agents don't allow their listing to go to Zillow. When you are looking online for houses for sale, you are most likely missing at least a few."

"I guess that makes sense," Mo said. "Should we look at the house?"

Ryan replied, "There may be another group in there looking at the house. This is an excellent deal, but we can look while they are looking."

Ryan gave Mo the MLS sheet so he could see all the details. This house was a four-level home. It was bigger than the other houses he had been looking at. Most of the other homes he saw were ranches with about 1,000 square feet on the main floor, and if they had a basement, another 1,000 square feet down there. This house had a main level that you walked up a few steps to get to. It had an upstairs with three bedrooms and two baths. It also had a lower level that had a family room with a fireplace, another bath, and a laundry room. The 2-car garage was also accessible from the lower level. There was a basement that connected to the family room from from another flight of stairs. The basement in this house was unfinished and had a furnace and hot water heater.

Mo could see why Ryan wanted him to look at this house so fast. It was listed for $129,900. The catch was the home was not in very good shape. It was built in 1972, and it looked like nothing had changed since it was built. There was light green shag carpet in the living room, orange carpet in the family room, and the bedrooms had blue, red, and purple carpet. There was hideous wallpaper everywhere and wood paneling all over the family room on the lower level. The kitchen had very old cabinets with a very old counter and an orange/blue vinyl floor. One bathroom upstairs had a pink tub, toilet, and sink, while the other had a light-blue toilet shower and sink. The lower level bath had a white toilet and sink, and that was about the only thing that was not stuck in the 1970's.

Mo looked at Ryan after seeing the house and said, "This place is freaking groovy man."

"Ha ha. Glad you like it. You know, some of this stuff is making a comeback," Ryan replied.

Mo asked, "Can I get a loan with all this work I have to do? I mean, it needs everything!"

Ryan replied, "Actually, yes. If you look at everything, it is just old and outdated. There is nothing that is broken. To get the FHA or conventional loan you want, this house would work great."

Mo said, "What about the cost to fix all of this up?! I don't have an unlimited amount of money to work with."

Ryan replied, "I know what you mean, but you can move in here and slowly fix things as you go. You can put in some sweat equity, and as you save money, make more repairs. The thing about this house is it may be worth $200,000 when it is fixed up."

Mo asked, "So why are they selling it so cheap?"

Ryan replied, "It is an estate sale. That means the person who owned the house died, and whoever inherited the house is trying to sell it. Estate sales can be great deals because the heirs just want to get rid of the home. What do you think? If you like it, we need to make an offer ASAP."

Mo was not happy about being pressured into making an offer. He had been waiting for the right house, and maybe this was it, but it needed so much work. He told Ryan he would go home and work on the numbers right away. Ryan had told him it would rent out for at least $1,600 a month if it was fixed up nicely. Mo knew those were some good numbers for a rental.

30

Is it a good deal?

Mo went home and ran the numbers on the property. It would make money as a rental. He knew that for sure. The big question was how much would it cost to fix it up? He figured it would be many thousands of dollars, even if he did the work himself. He was not sure he wanted to commit to such a huge undertaking.

Ryan had made some more good points while they were touring the home. He had mentioned that you do not have to make a rental property perfect to get it rented out. If he was going to sell the house and try to get top dollar, he would need to repair and replace much of the house, but as a rental, he would not have to do nearly as much.

Ryan also said that this was such a good deal Mo could probably sell it without making any repairs and make a profit. The sellers wanted it sold fast, and that was why they were willing to sell it so cheap.

Mo had a lot to think about. He also had just enough money to buy this property if the sellers were willing to pay his closing costs for him. He was not sure they would do that if they wanted the house sold so fast.

Ryan had assured him it was still worth making an offer, and if they got their offer in right away, the seller may accept it before other offers came in. Mo was still hesitant and not sure what to do. Was this the right house for him?

Ryan sent him another text that night asking if Mo had gone over the numbers. Mo took his time replying because he was not sure what to say. He had gone over the numbers. It was an awesome deal, but he was not sure what to do. He finally responded to Ryan 30 minutes later and told him he had to sleep on it.

Mo was hoping that he would wake up knowing what to do, but he was just as confused as the previous night. He had to go to work and decided to keep thinking about the deal. He was waiting for Ryan to text him again, but he never did. Mo kept thinking about the house all day while he was working. He was getting ready to head home for the day when he finally made a decision.

He would make an offer on the house. He had enough money. It was an awesome deal, much better than anything else he had seen. It was also a cool house, and it would be interesting living with shag carpet until he could afford to replace it. After all, he had just gotten a raise.

He texted Ryan and told him sorry it took so long but wants to make an offer.

Ryan called Mo back right away.

"Hey Ryan. What's up?"

"I wanted to call and let you know that house already went under contract. Sorry to give you the bad news, but those good deals go fast."

Mo felt his stomach drop. He knew it was a good deal but thought Ryan was being a little too pushy with making an offer right away. Apparently, Ryan was right. "Oh" was all Mo could say.

Ryan replied, "Don't worry. There will be more deals and houses out there. This could be a good learning experience for you, and we know there is a house that would work for you as well. We will keep looking."

Mo was disappointed. He had finally convinced himself that this was the right house, and now it was gone. He knew there was a chance he still would not have gotten the house if he made an offer, but he would have liked to at least try.

Ryan told him the house may come back on the market if the buyer doesn't like the inspection, which happens a lot on these houses, but Mo was sure he had lost it.

He could not do anything about the house now. He had asked Ryan what it sold for, but Ryan said he would not know what the contract price was until it actually sold, which could be 2 to 4 weeks from now.

Mo was hoping it sold for much more than he wanted to offer. That way he would not feel bad about missing out on this one since he would not have gotten it anyway.

31

There will be more

Mo went to work the next day very disappointed—almost depressed. He felt like he had messed up...badly. He had hesitated on a really good deal and a really cool house. He could hope that it fell apart, but he did not think it would. The other person would be stupid not to buy that house.

He could not do anything about it now, and he knew he should not let missing the house bother him so much, but it did. He managed to get through work without really talking to anyone. That was nice. he could wallow in his own thoughts of "what if."

Ryan had talked to him and told him there would be more houses and not to get upset about missing this one. Ryan told Mo that it takes most people a couple of tries before they get a house. It is rare they buy the first one they like or offer on. In a market where houses move quickly, buyers must move quickly as well. Ryan was especially clear that Mo would have to move more quickly than most buyers because he was looking for an awesome deal. As Mo had found out, the great deals are not just sitting on the MLS waiting for someone to snag them.

Mo got home and looked through the listings on Zillow. He did not find anything that looked amazing. He found a few decent deals, but they needed a lot more work than he was willing to or could do. They were similar to the houses that Ryan had showed him a few weeks ago. Now he was really depressed because he realized this was the first house that he could see himself living in that was a good deal. He had hesitated and missed it!

Alright. Mo decided he needed to stop dwelling on the house. He thought about what else he could do to take his mind off it. He could read more real estate books. No, that would definitely not take his mind off it.

He could work out! Whenever he worked out, he felt better about himself and his life. He was wondering why he did not work out more, but that was something else he did not want to think about at the moment.

He pulled out the limited workout equipment he had in his apartment and went to work.

30 minutes or so later, he was feeling much better about himself. He was still thinking a little bit about the house, but he knew there would be more houses in the future. To be honest, he was not sure he had quite enough money to buy that house yet anyway. He was saving, but that house was a little more than he hoped to pay. Plus, he would have had to find money to fix it up at some point. That was assuming he even got his offer accepted had he made one. He was having doubts he would have gotten the house, even if he had tried. An investor could have swooped in with a cash offer, and no matter what Mo offered, he may not have gotten it.

He was finally breaking out of his funk and feeling better about himself. Life was not over. He could find more houses, and he would buy a house at some point!

32

Another opportunity

A couple more weeks passed with nothing exciting happening. Mo continued to look for houses that came up for sale. Ryan would also email him new listings that he thought might work. They went and saw a couple of houses, but they both knew they were not right for Mo. One of the houses only had 2 bedrooms, and while Mo did not need more than that, he wanted at least a three bedroom to rent out.

The other house they looked at was not in bad shape, but it was simply priced too high for Mo. He was doing his best to be patient, but it was not easy!

Then, on a on a Wednesday, Ryan called Mo (which was strange because he always texted) and told him an interesting property had come up for sale. The house was a HUD home and a great deal. Mo had vaguely heard of HUD but was not quite sure how they worked.

Ryan told Mo how HUD homes worked, but it all sounded very confusing. They were a type of foreclosure owned by the government, and the government would auction them off. Ryan said that HUD homes are nice for people in his situation because they give precedence to people who are going to be owner occupants. Since Mo was going to live in the house for at least one year, he would qualify as an owner occupant.

Ryan continued to tell Mo about HUD homes. "Many HUD homes are great deals but need a little work. They can be an amazing opportunity for owner occupants because HUD wants owner occupants to buy them. Investors are not even allowed to bid until owner occupants have been given a chance to purchase the home."

Ryan kept going, "The downside is that HUD will not make any repairs or fix any items on a property. So many times the houses cannot qualify for financing because they need too much work. However, HUD works closely with FHA loans because FHA loans are government backed and HUD is a government entity."

Ryan said that if Mo were to get an FHA loan on a HUD property, that did not need too much work, there is a program that allows him to finance repairs if they are less than $5,000. Mo would not have to get the 203K rehab loan, which is usually a difficult loan to work with.

Mo was hoping to get a conventional loan because the rates were cheaper and the closing cost were lower than FHA. He could also remove mortgage insurance on a conventional loan after a couple of years. However, he knew that if he found the right deal an FHA loan, would work as well.

Ryan told Mo about the property, which was listed for a $114,900. The property was in an area that Mo knew. It needed some work but was not a full rehab. The property was about 30 years old, so it should have fairly decent bones and hopefully needed only cosmetic work to bring it up to Mo's standards, not that he had crazy high standards, but he did have some.

Ryan thought the home would rent out for $1,400 a month, maybe a little more if it was fixed up. He also thought the home would be worth more than a $150,000 once it was repaired if Mo ever wanted to sell it or refinance it.

This sounded like the deal Mo had been waiting for, and he could not wait to see the property. He did not want to get his hopes up, but maybe he had found his house.

It had taken a while, and this house was not as cool as the last house that he wanted to offer on, but the house was cheaper, looked like it needed less work, and might be a better fit for Mo.

33

What is HUD?

Mo wanted to set up an appointment with Ryan as soon as possible. Ryan was not in a huge hurry to meet him, which was bugging him. He did not want to lose this house! But then Ryan explained why he was in no hurry. HUD homes have a 10-day bid period for owner-occupied buyers. So, Mo could make his offer any time in the first 10 days, and it would not give him any better or worse chance of getting the property than if he made his offer on the first day.

Mo relaxed a little bit and decided to go see the house when it was convenient for Ryan. Ryan had found the house for him and had been a tremendous help. He decided he did not need to go see the house that very second.

Mo was at work and really excited about seeing the house. He had an urge to tell someone about it and that this could be the house for him. There was only one person he could talk to about houses at work, and that was Sarah.

Mo had not talked to her much since she seemed less than thrilled with his promotion. He had mentioned this to one of the other guys at work on Monday evening when they went out to dinner. He had told Mo that Sarah was very serious about her job and wanted to get a manager position herself. She was probably annoyed that Mo got to manager so quickly. Mo could understand that. The biggest reason he was able to become a manager was that they had no IT manager. He was not even sure that he was being much of a manager, but Tory seemed happy.

Mo strolled over to Sarah's desk and told her about the house. She seemed genuinely excited about it and much more talkative. Maybe she was just having a bad day before or she had gotten over the manager thing.

They talked a little bit, and he asked her to go to lunch with him. He had done some research and did not find any specific rules against dating a coworker. He was still not in love with her by any means, but he liked hanging out with her, and she was very smart. They had lunch, talked a lot, and things seemed to go just fine.

Mo was still not sure what he thought about Sarah, but he knew he wanted to take whatever it was slowly. He was making a lot of life changes and wanted a clear head. He thought Sarah was cool, but he did not know her that well. They mostly small talked. He figured if he wanted to take the next step, he would need to ask her out on a real date, but he was not sure he wanted to. He was also not sure if he didn't want to ask her because of everything else that was going on or if it was because he was scared. He decided that was too deep of a conversation to have with himself and tried to think of something else. He would deal with that line of thinking later.

An excruciating two days later, Mo met Ryan at the HUD home. The property was ugly on the outside, just like Mo had imagined his first house would be. The yard was dead and the outside needed some paint. Mo was used to properties that needed some work, and these cosmetic items did not scare him. He was not worried about doing a little work, but he was worried about getting his loan.

The outside of the house needing paint worried him because he had heard that houses with peeling paint could not get conventional or FHA loans. Ryan reminded Mo that HUD had a program for FHA loans and they could actually escrow those repairs. Mo remembered Ryan saying a lot about HUD homes, but he could understand half of it, and he remembered even less. He didn't actually know what escrow meant, but he didn't want to tell Ryan that. He would look it up later.

Mo opened the door to the house with excitement. He wanted to see what his new house might look like. He walked into the living room. The home had a very similar floor plan to the first house he saw with Ryan that smelled so bad. Many of the houses he saw had very similar floor plans, as they were very popular in the 1960s and 1970,s. The living room had hardwood floors. It opened into the dining room where the hardwood continued, and the dining room opened into the kitchen.

The living space on the main floor was not bad at all. The hardwood was scratched up and very dull, but Ryan said it could be refinished. The paint was fading, and the walls were very dirty, but he saw no holes. The windows were aluminum, which Ryan said was not the best for energy efficiency, but none of them were broken.

The house had light fixtures from the 1990s. They were bright gold brass, and Mo thought they were god-awful ugly. The kitchen cabinets were older but solid wood and white. It looked like the cabinets were a darker color at one time, but an owner along the way had painted them. They did not have any fancy shaker design like the newer cabinets had. They were pretty much flat wood panels, but they were not in bad condition. The counter tops were not amazing. They were a pale yellow that had once been white and stained over the years...or a brighter yellow that had dulled over the years. They were laminate and had a lot of edges with chipping and peeling pieces. He knew the counters would have to go. The stove was missing, but there was a dishwasher. He guessed it had not worked for many years, but at least there was a space for it. A few of the houses Mo had looked had no dishwashers at all or space to put them. The fridge was gone as well.

Mo went back through the kitchen and dining room to the three upstairs bedrooms. They all had old carpet, but they could see where someone had pulled up the carpet and the carpet pad beneath to see if the bedrooms had hardwood. Mo and Ryan looked, and there was more hardwood! That meant the entire main floor most likely had hardwood.

The doors were there, but they were flat panel and wood that had a lot of cracks and a few holes. Ryan said he would want new doors for sure since they would really update the house.

There was one bathroom on the main floor, and it was not horrible but not amazing either. The toilet, sink, and tub were a baby blue/pastel. Mo realized the house was built in the 1970s, and people had some weird design choices back then, but the blue and pink bathroom fixtures he kept finding in houses baffled him.

After looking at the first floor, he could not find any major problems with the house. He reminded himself he was not a professional investor yet and did not know everything he should be looking for. There was also the basement, which usually held the scary stuff in these houses.

He walked downstairs, following Ryan. He found the basement was neglected but nothing he could not handle. They walked into the family room that had older brown and black splotchy carpet, 30-year-old light fixtures, wood paneling on the walls, and an old bar that was straight out of the 1970s. It was not a wet bar, but the bar had a giant wood top that sat on what looked like black leather couch cushions. It was cool, but Mo could not decide if it was cool enough to stay in the house if he ended up getting it.

On one end of the family room was a bedroom with a tiny window. Mo asked, "Don't I need to have an egress window for this to be a real bedroom?"

Ryan responded, "Technically, you can say the basement was finished before that code came into effect, which means the bedroom was grandfathered in with the smaller window. That does not mean you cannot put an egress window in the bedroom, and if you are going to use it as a rental, that might be a good idea."

Mo thought about that while he looked at the rest of the bedroom, which had the same carpet as the family room and the same wood paneling, but someone had painted it white at some point in the house's life. The bedroom did have a closet, but the closet doors were missing.

Mo walked back into the family room where he found a hallway back by the stairs. He found a bathroom to one side of the hallway. The bathroom needed paint as well and had a very old toilet and vanity. They were pink! Mo also found a small shower that was tiled with square white tiles, but it looked like it had not been used for many years.

They walked out of the bathroom and found another bedroom which looked a lot like the first bedroom they saw in the basement with the tiny window. Ryan guided Mo back out of the bedroom and the end of the hall where they found the laundry and utility room. Ryan showed him the furnace and the water heater, although Mo had no idea what he was looking at. Ryan seemed to think the water heater was more than 10 years old, which meant it might need to be replaced. And he said the furnace was about 15 years old, which meant it could be okay or could need to be replaced depending on how well it had been maintained.

The laundry room had an unfinished ceiling, so Mo could see wires and pipes in the floor joists. Ryan showed him some of the pipes while they were in the laundry room. He told him that galvanized pipes and nob-and-tube wiring were bad. Mo nodded and pretended to know what Ryan was talking about. Mo made a note to research these things when he got back to his apartment.

Ryan and Mo headed back upstairs and found the door to the garage was right at the top of the stairway. They walked into the garage and found enough room for one car. The floor was smooth concrete, and the walls had no drywall except for the wall that was attached to the house. Mo could see the roof trusses in the ceiling as there was no drywall there either.

They walked through the garage to a door that lead to the backyard. The grass was dead. There was a small concrete patio behind the house with some cracks in it, an old tree, and a chain link fence. Mo could see the back of the house, which was brick. Brick was great for exterior maintenance because it never needed painting, although trim around the roof and windows would need paint. The house had older windows, but none of them were broken, and Mo thought he could live with the older aluminum windows, at least for now.

It was interesting for Mo to look at this house because he had to think of it as something he would live in and something that would eventually be an investment property. He thought he could definitely live here. It was not as nice as his apartment, but the mortgage payment would actually be lower than his rent was now. He could make the property nice enough for him to live in, and it would be his property.

Mo knew he could do some of the painting and other minor repairs himself. He was not a professional and really had no idea how to do any of these repairs, but he also knew YouTube taught you just about everything.

On the investment side of the property, Mo thought it had a ton of potential. The house had 5 bedrooms, which was great for resale. It would rent out for a decent amount at $1,400 a month. When he ran all the numbers, he would make money on the property even with his mortgage insurance. Not only would he make money on the rent, but he would come away with $20,000 to $30,000 in instant equity depending on what he got the house for.

Mo knew he wanted to make an offer on his house and hopefully make it his first property. The question now was how much should he offer?

34

Don't mess around

M o thanked Ryan for showing him the property and told him he would run some numbers and think about the place back at his apartment. Mo really wanted to go over everything while the house was fresh in his head. He did not have to worry about making an offer right away on a HUD home, which was nice. No bids would be accepted before the 10-day bid period was up.

Mo got back to his apartment and knew it was time to crunch numbers to see what the property would make if he rented it out. He decided to base his numbers off a full-price offer on the home:

Purchase price: $115,000 (rounded up to make it easier)
   Mortgage payment: $595.74 based on a 5% interest rate
   Down payment: $4,025 with FHA's 3.5% requirement.

Mo could live with these numbers, but he barely had enough money saved for the down payment, and he had not included the closing costs yet. He was thinking it was probably a good thing he did not get his offer accepted on that other house! He also knew that his payment would be much higher than $595 once he included taxes, insurance, and mortgage insurance.

Ryan had mentioned HUD was willing to pay the closing costs for buyers, which meant he only needed the down-payment money. Ryan also mentioned that HUD determined the winning bid based on the net amount of money HUD received. If Mo asked for $3,000 in closing costs, his offer would be $3,000 lower in the eyes of HUD. He would lose out to another bidder with the same bid as him if they did not ask for closing costs.

The property taxes were about $1,500 a year, and insurance would be about $700 a year.

The mortgage insurance was a killer on FHA loans though. Mo would have to pay 1.75 % of the loan amount up front and .85% of the loan amount every year. The monthly payment would increase $80 a month because off the mortgage insurance, and he would need another $1,942 for mortgage insurance up front. The nice thing about the upfront mortgage insurance was it could be included in his loan, so he did not have to come up with that cash.

His payment would be:

Insurance: $58

Taxes: $125

Mortgage: $596

MI: $80

Total: $859

That payment was not bad, but he knew there would be more costs with the house. He would have vacancies and maintenance once he rented it out. Those costs could add another $200 to $300 month, but he was still making money if it rented out for $1,400 a month. In fact, he was making pretty good money considering he was also walking into a lot of equity. Later on down the road, he might be able to refinance the property and get rid of the mortgage insurance.

The house was a great deal, and it would be a great rental once he fixed it up and lived there for a year. Mo had decided he would make an offer on the home, but he had to decide how much to offer.

35

Just do it

The house was listed for $114,900, and Ryan told Mo he may have to offer more to get the house, especially if he was going to ask HUD to pay the closing costs. Mo decided to head over to Ryan's office so they could go over everything in person.

After Mo and Ryan talked for a while, Mo decided to make an offer of $118,750 and see what happened. He was going to ask for 3% in closing costs, which should cover most of the costs besides the down payment. Mo wanted to make sure his offer was slightly more than the listing price. By asking for 3% in closing costs ($3,562.50) and offering $118,750, he was basically making an offer of $115,187.50. Just in case there was another buyer who was going to offer full price, Mo offered a little more to beat them out.

Mo was worried that his financing would hurt him against other buyers. He knew that some sellers preferred buyers with conventional mortgages instead of FHA mortgages. He also knew that most sellers preferred cash offers with no financing contingencies. Mo asked Ryan about this, and Ryan said that HUD does not care. They look at a cash offer the same way they look at an FHA offer. The only thing they consider when picking an offer is the net price to them.

Mo was super excited and was ready to offer on the house. Ryan reminded him of the escrow they had talked about earlier. Mo had completely forgotten about the escrow and still had no idea how it worked.

Ryan said that HUD will escrow minor repairs on some of their properties if the buyer uses an FHA loan. If the buyer uses any other type of financing, the escrow cannot be used. An appraiser that HUD hires comes up with an amount they feel it will take to fix the items that will get the home up to FHA standards. On this house, the escrow amount was $2,200. HUD listed $1,500 for exterior paint and $700 for plumbing. The escrow did not include flooring or replacing the outdated item—just repairs that a loan would require to be done.

Mo was excited that HUD was going to give him this money to fix up the house, but Ryan told him that was not how it worked. HUD would add the money to Mo's loan and hold it in escrow account to pay the person who did the work on the house. HUD does not allow any work to be done before closing, and this system allows a buyer to get an FHA loan on a house that would otherwise not qualify for the loan. The escrow allowed the loan to go through, but Mo was still paying for the repairs.

At least he would not have to come up with the cash for those repairs because the money was added to his loan. If he had bought the other house, he would have had to come up with all the money to make the repairs.

The other issue that Mo faced was the plumbing. Ryan explained that the HUD inspectors (HUD does an inspection on all of their houses before they list them) found plumbing leaks when they did an air test on the plumbing system. HUD does not turn on the water before they do their inspection, so they perform an air test to see if it holds pressure. If the system does not hold pressure, it means there is a leak somewhere. Sometimes, the HUD inspectors can tell where the leak is, and sometimes they cannot.

Ryan apologized and said he should have looked at the escrow repair items before they saw the house, but he completely forgot about them.

The escrow document said HUD detected a leak somewhere in the system, and they estimated it would cost $700 to fix. Ryan told Mo that they could not rely on that report, and the leaks could be more expensive or less expensive to fix. The other kicker was that Mo would not be allowed to turn on the water for his inspection either. If HUD finds the system does not hold pressure, they do not allow the water to be turned on. HUD does not want the buyer flooding the house.

Ryan went over more of the numbers with him. He said that HUD works a little differently than most sellers. HUD will not pay for title insurance like most sellers do, but that could be paid by the closing costs that Mo asked to be paid. HUD also does not pay for any of the utilities to be turned on for inspections. Most houses already have the utilities turned on because people are living there or recently moved. However, many bank-owned foreclosures and HUD homes turn the utilities off. They do not want the pipes freezing in the winter, breaking and flooding the home. Ryan told him that many banks will pay for the utilities to be turned on for inspections, but HUD will not. Not only did Mo have to pay for the utilities to be turned on, but he had to pay for any usage of those utilities. Ryan told Mo that, in some cases, he would have to pay for the home to be winterized again after his inspection. Since he was not able to turn on the water, he was able to avoid that cost, which was around $150.

Mo's head was spinning with all this information, but Ryan told him it was actually a simple process once you understood how it worked. He explained that banks and HUD winterize their homes when they turn the utilities off. When they winterize a home, they blow all the water out of the pipes, put antifreeze in the toilets and sinks, and drain the water heaters. If he was doing a full inspection with the water on, he would have to de-winterize the home. That meant you turn the water on and watch everything like a hawk for leaks. Once you were done with the inspection, you would need to have a plumber winterize the home again.

Mo would not have to pay for the winterization, but the costs kept adding up on this property, and Mo was wondering if it was even worth it to buy a HUD home. Then, he remembered how many houses he had seen and how perfect this one was, at least for him. He chuckled to himself thinking that most buyers would think this house was the opposite of perfect because of the work it needed.

He decided to move forward with the offer and trust that Ryan knew what he was talking about. He could still get out of the deal if the inspection was horrible or revealed some major problems with the home.

Mo was glad he had an awesome agent who understood all of this. He could not imagine how lost he would be with some of the other agents he had first met who had no clue about what he was trying to do.

Mo and Ryan were ready to submit the contract to HUD. Mo was excited to see his first contract. Ryan had told him about contracts and how they worked, but Mo had not actually seen one yet. Unfortunately, HUD had another surprise for him. He did not have to sign a contract to submit a bid to HUD. Ryan would submit all the information online, and if his bid was accepted, he would have 48 hours to send all the documents to HUD.

It took Ryan about 3 minutes to enter the information for Mo. Mo could not believe how simple it was, and Ryan reminded him again that HUD does things much differently than other sellers.

Ryan asked, "Are you ready to send in your first offer? Once I hit this submit button, it will go to HUD...and we wait."

"Do it!" Mo replied

Ryan clicked on the "Confirm Your Bid" button on the computer screen, and the offer was sent to HUD. Now, Mo had to wait a few days until the initial biding period was up to see if he was the winning bidder.

Mo headed back home and could not believe he just made his first offer on a house. He was hoping he would get to at least sign something, but Ryan submitted everything online for him. Mo could not believe the government was using so much technology!

Mo had a hard time sitting still or concentrating on anything at home. He had no way of knowing if he would have the high bid until the first 10 days had passed and HUD received all the owner-occupied offers. That was still almost a week away. Mo had asked Ryan if there was any way they could find out what the other offers were, and Ryan said no. Even the agent who lists the house for HUD does not know what offers were submitted until HUD picks a winner. And then they are only notified of the winning bid.

For the first time ever, Mo was excited to go to work. He needed something to take his mind off of the house.

36

You can't wait for things to happen

The next day, Mo was back at work, still excited about the offer he had made on the HUD home. The offer and process of making the offer had jogged something loose inside of him. His mind kept drifting to his career and whether he wanted to stay in his job.

Mo had a few more responsibilities with his promotion, but it was nothing he could not handle. He was severely underutilized at work. He could do so much with websites and computers, but he was stuck doing tech service. His job was much better since he adopted his new attitude, but he still knew he could be doing a lot more with his skills. Even as a manager, he was not challenged on the computer side of things. He thought he would be challenged on the people-managing side of it since he had never done that before. However, there was not much managing to do either.

In the past, he would have been scared to take on something new, but he had taken on real estate, and while he had not technically bought a house yet, he knew he would. He knew almost nothing about real estate when he started but had learned an incredible amount in the last few months. With the right attitude and motivation, he knew he could learn management as well . Yet, while he could learn it, he was not very excited about it. He was excited about real estate. He was wondering if he was on the right track with his career or if he should be thinking about something else.

The tough thing about work was that he needed the job to get a loan. He had to have steady employment with a solid work history to get a conventional or FHA mortgage. For the time being, he was going to stay at his job and make the best of it.

Mo had some down time at work that morning, and he began to contemplate his career. He had first taken this job because it had something to do with computers and it paid decently. He knew computers very well. He loved them, and it seemed like a great fit for him. However, the job was simple tech support and nothing challenging. He wasn't really working with computers. Anyone with basic knowledge of them could do this job.

Thinking back on when he got the job, he realized he had not even thought that much about his career. He was not very thorough or selective when searching for a job to make sure the job fit him well. If he had been smart about it, he would have looked for companies that fit him, not simply looked for any job that was available. He realized he never really knew how to get a job except the way he had done it.

From his reading and learning over the last few months, Mo had realized that you have to go after what you want—it will not come to you. When Mo decided he wanted to invest in real estate, a house had not simply shown up in his email one day and said "buy me." He had to do a lot of work to figure out how to invest and what to invest in, and then he had to find that investment. The perfect job would not land in your lap after looking in the classifieds for a couple of weeks either. But that was all he had done to get this job.

Mo had not tried very hard to find a job that suited him. He had settled for something that was quick and easy. He knew the job was not perfect for him when he first got it, but he had told himself he would stay for a little while until he established himself. Then with some experience and work history, he could look for that perfect job. He had settled into the job, but he had not done much besides that.

He was beginning to realize that while he was having more fun at his job, it was not the best fit for him. He needed something that would challenge him and that would be fun. Who knows—maybe at some point he could even start his own business.

He was not ready to start his own business yet, but he decided he would start to think about his career more. He had planned out a better future with real estate, and he would plan out a better future with work as well. Now, he just had to figure out how he would do that. Luckily he had plenty of energy and time while he waited for the answer on his first house.

It was time to go to work on improving his career. It would not happen by itself.

37

What is right for me?

Mo figured that he would take the same approach on his career as he took with real estate. He would do some reading and research to find out what he should do. He started online and realized that there were thousands of articles on how to pick the right career. He also noticed that the marketing was not quite as intense as it was with real estate investing sites.

With real estate, it seemed like most the articles were an advertisement for a coaching program. With the career articles, there were fewer articles trying to sell things. He liked the articles that did not try to sell anything better, but he also wondered how they made money compared to the real estate sites that offered coaching. Mo figured they had advertising and affiliate sales to make money. An affiliate sale is when a site sent you to another site to buy something. If you bought something at the other site, the first site would get a percentage of the sale for referring you there. He had almost become blind to the ads on articles because he saw so many of them. You get used to scrolling past the ads, and if they are too overwhelming, you simply look for a new article.

The trouble with so many articles on careers was there were so many opinions on what to do. Some said you should do what you love while others said you should follow the money. Some articles talked about taking personality tests and aptitude tests to find what you were good at. A few articles talked about starting your business while others focused on a corporate career.

Mo felt similar to how he felt when he first started researching real estate. He was overwhelmed and a little lost. He did not know who to believe or where to start. He remembered that it took some time with real estate, but he eventually figured it out. He kept reading, kept researching, and assumed things would become clearer.

Things did clear up after a few days of immersing himself in articles. There were a lot of opinions, but he decided to listen to the things that made sense to him. He tried to be wary of the get-rich-quick schemes or the sounds-too-good-to-be-true offers.

A few things stood out to him.

He needed to do something that he loved. There were a few opinions on this subject, but doing something that you loved made sense. If you love your work, you are happier, you don't need motivation, and you don't get burned out as easily. A few people said that if you dread Mondays because you have to work, you need to find a new job or line of work. Mo did not dread Mondays, but he certainly did not look forward to them.

If you do something that you love, you will automatically be motivated to work harder at your job. You will have fun at work, and you will naturally be willing to work harder because it is enjoyable. If you dislike your job, you can motivate yourself to work hard and go above and beyond. However, you probably only think about that job when you have to. You are stressed because you don't enjoy it, and your only motivation is money. Most people burn out pretty quick when they are doing something they do not like. Or, they half-ass their way through the work and wonder why nothing much comes of it. That seemed a little familiar to Mo.

Another theme that Mo saw over and over in the articles was starting a business. Many people did not start a business right off the bat. But, they went to work in a field they loved, they learned all they could about that field, and then they started their own company. Sometimes they quit their job and went all in with the new company, and sometimes they started it on the side and grew it until it was big enough to quit their day job.

Could Mo ever quit his job? Could he find something that suited him better or start his own business? Starting a business seemed overwhelming, but it also excited him. He had never really thought about starting a business. In fact he was always a little jealous of people who did have their own business. He wondered how they got so lucky to make their own schedule, hire the people they wanted, and make big money.

Mo knew they were not lucky, but they had more guts than most people. They were willing to do what most people are not willing to do, which is take chances and risk financial stability. Maybe one day, Mo could be one of those business owners as well. That felt good to think about.

38

A new business

Mo was at the office getting used to his new manager position. It was not tough, and he mostly still did the same stuff he did before. The only difference was the other guys in the office had to report to him. He kept track of what they were working on and made sure they were actually working.

He could not get too mad at them if they weren't working all the time as there really was not that much work to be done. Mo had messed around a lot at work and still managed to get all of his responsibilities taken care of. Mo did like being able to send them to a job that he would normally have to go to. Tory had told him not to be afraid to delegate a few tasks.

Mo was also worried that the other guys might be jealous that he got the manager position. However, he quickly found out they did not care. They were both introverts and did not want anything to do with being a manager.

Mo still had another day to wait until he heard if he had gotten the HUD house or not. He was trying to keep himself occupied by thinking about his work situation instead of thinking about the house. He could not do anything about it except wait. Well actually, Ryan said that he could raise his offer if he wanted to up until the bid submission deadline. However, Mo had decided to leave his offer where it was and see what happened.

Mo still could not get the idea out of his head that he needed to change something about his work. He was enjoying it more, but it was not challenging him at all. He had an idea what he wanted to do, but he was not sure how he would accomplish it. He loved computers, and he loved working online. He did not love tech support or the technical side of the business. Maybe he did not even love computers, but he loved what they could do.

Mo had thought about creating a proposal for Tory to redo the entire system at the company. However, Mo had never gotten around to it. He was beginning to think there was a reason he did not get around to that project. It did not feel right. Yes, it would be more challenging, help the company, and be slightly more difficult than the work he was doing now, but it still would not be that fun or he would have done it already.

While Mo was researching real estate and careers, he had a lot of fun and interest analyzing the different websites he went to and books he read. He liked to see how the different experts in the field marketed themselves. It was also fun to see how the real estate guys marketed themselves compared to the big websites that were more about advertising.

Maybe marketing was something that he could be good at and that would go hand-in-hand with his computer skills. He was not sure how good of a marketer he was, but he loved seeing all the different techniques out there. He knew which techniques he liked the best and which ones he hated. He also knew that some of the techniques he hated most likely made the most money. That was a conundrum, especially if you are working for someone else. Do you market in a way that is fair to the consumer but may limit the earnings of your boss or the site you are trying to improve? Or, do you maximize the profits for the person that pays you and not worry so much about the consumer?

He knew what the answer was for the real estate seminars he attended. They maximized profit without seeming to care at all about the consumer. Or, maybe they justified it by feeling the end justifies the means. Sure, these people are spending $30,000 on coaching, but they will learn how to flip houses that will make them ten times that amount of money.

The problem Mo had was that most of those people were never going to flip a house or by spending $30,000 on a coaching program. They were digging themselves into a huge hole that many would never get out of. Even Mo, who was better off than most, would have been in a huge hole if he would have shelled out that much money. He was able to learn from books, blogs, YouTube, and local people like his real estate agent.

If he would have spent $30,000 on a coaching program, he would have never qualified for the loan he was trying to get. Who knows how long it would have taken him to save up the money for his down payment. He would have had no choice but to stop going out with his buddies because there was no other way he could pay back that money. He was still a little strapped for cash, but he was much better off than he would have been.

It is funny where your mind takes you when you sit down and let it think about things without distractions. Mo decided that internet marketing may be what he wanted to do with his life, but he had no idea where to start. He was pretty sure he was not going to find an add on Craigslist asking for a digital or internet marketer with no marketing experience.

He also wanted to make sure he bought his first house before he did anything drastic with his job. He did not want to screw up the loan. The lender had been very clear that he needed a good job history, keep his job, and not buy anything crazy like a new car because that could screw up the loan as well.

That did not mean he could not start working on marketing in his free time or start a side business. He knew he would have some time and energy to kill once he bought his first house. He could not move out and rent out that house until he had lived there for at least one year. During that year, he could work on his career.

39

Did I get it?

Today was the day that Mo would learn if he got the HUD home. He was trying not to get his hopes up. He had started this process a few months ago, and this was the first house he had submitted an offer on. He could not expect to get the first house he offered on, could he? It would be great if he did, but he was not going to be devastated if it did not work out. Even if Mo did get his contract accepted, he still had to get the loan and get through the inspection. It would not be a done deal.

Ryan had told him that it might take until noon to get an answer from HUD, but it could be sooner. Mo was at work and had a few things to do, but he was having a hard time concentrating. Sarah knew that he would find out today if he got the house, and she had already found him and told him good luck and that she was rooting for him.

It had felt good to have her support and have a few friends at the office.

They had seen each other again for lunch, but they had not gone on an official date or talked about dating at all. Mo had decided to take things slowly, especially with everything else that was going on in his life. He had some huge life changes going on as well as some big decisions to make. He figured he did not need to complicate things with a girlfriend right now. At the same time, he was not going to rule her out or push her away. At least, that was his plan. He knew things did not always happen how you thought they would in the world of romance.

Right around 10, Ryan sent him a text message. Mo saw who it was from but was scared to look at the message. He did not want to see a message that said, "Sorry we did not get it, but don't worry—we will keep trying." He was also a little worried about getting a message that said, "Congrats! You got it!". He took a few minutes longer than he should have to finish up some work then decided it was time to see what Ryan had said.

He peaked at his phone, opened up the text and read, "Hey Mo. I will be sure to let you know as soon as I hear anything."

Seriously? Ryan had the nerve to send a text without any news? The suspense was killing him! All that build up and he still did not have an answer. He would have to keep plugging away at work and try not to think about the house every five seconds.

About 15 minutes later, Mo got another text, and it was Ryan again. He decided to stop being a baby and just look at the message this time. He opened up the message and it read, "You are the winning bidder of a HUD home!"

Mo could not believe it. He had gotten the bid! There was still work to be done, but he had actually gotten an offer accepted on a property, and it was his first offer! Now he had to get his earnest money together. HUD required a certified check for earnest money, and Mo only had a day to get all the paperwork and documents to Ryan to send off to HUD.

He went to the bank on his lunch break to get the check. He had not felt this excited or happy about anything for a long time. He was also a little scared—well, to be honest, a lot scared—but it was a good scared. He knew he was in for an adventure, and he was starting to do something with his life.

40

Now it gets real

After getting the cashiers check from the bank, which was for $1,000, Mo went back to work but had set up a time to meet with Ryan after he got off. He did not get much accomplished that afternoon, but he did tell Sarah his offer was accepted and she seemed super excited for him.

Mo headed to Ryan's office after work. He had to be careful not to speed the entire way there. When he got to Ryan's brokerage, he met the receptionist, who was leaving for the day, and she told him to head back to Ryan's office.

Mo saw Ryan and could not help but give him a hearty handshake and a half hug. Ryan told him, "Congrats! There was no way I thought you would be buying a house this quickly. Most of the other investors I work with take a long time to take the plunge and buy their first property!"

"It surprised me too man. I can't believe I have come this far after a few short months. It is crazy to think back to where I was hanging out with my friends and doing nothing with my life to being here now," Mo replied.

Mo thought he would have a ton of paperwork to sign after all he had read on buying a house. He thought it would be even worse with a government-owned home. He was wrong. The contract was only one page long, although he did have a few disclosures to sign.

The disclosures said he had to live in the house as an owner occupant, said HUD would not make any repairs, and discussed how the inspection and earnest money worked.

With most houses, the buyer had a chance to do their inspection and cancel the contract if the seller would not fix what the buyers asked to be fixed.

With HUD, the inspection is similar. However, investors only get their earnest money back if their loan is denied, and in that case they may only get half their earnest money back. Owner occupants usually will get all of their earnest money back if the inspection is not acceptable as long as the reason they're canceling was not already in HUD's inspection report. HUD provides an inspection report for every property, and if a repair is listed in that report, the buyers are expected to already know about it when they make their offer.

Mo peeked at the inspection provided by HUD. Ryan had told him what was on the escrow repair sheet, but he had not seen the inspection report yet. He knew what he thought was wrong with the property, but he wanted to see what HUD had to say as well. Mo was also going to get his own inspection to make sure nothing else was wrong. Ryan had told him that HUD's inspectors are not very reliable, and he definitely needed to get his own inspection done.

Mo was not too worried about the inspection report right now. He was worried about getting all the paperwork signed and his earnest money and pre-qualification all sent into HUD. Ryan told him to look at the inspection report anyway because he could not get his earnest money back if they cancelled due to an item already on that report.

The inspection report was only one page long and had almost no information on it. It mentioned the furnace seemed to be in good visual shape but that the inspector never turned it on. It said the electric system seemed to be fine. It also mentioned there was a plumbing leak somewhere in the house, but the inspector had no idea where that leak was. The report also mentioned that the roof appeared to be in decent shape. And that was about it. Mo looked at Ryan, "This is all they tell you? I thought an inspection would be a little more thorough."

Ryan chuckled and said, "I told you this is a HUD inspection. It is not even close to what a real inspection report will look like, and this is why I have been telling you to get your own inspection on this house."

Mo replied,"Got it. Makes sense now, but you would think HUD would put a little more effort into things!"

Mo was fine with the report as there was nothing in it that he did not already know. Ryan said that HUD was very particular about the paperwork, the earnest money, and his pre-qualification letter being perfect. After going through all this to find a house and get the offer accepted, they did not want to screw something up.

Mo signed the one-page contract, which literally had like ten things on it. It was crazy that HUD had such simple paperwork since they're a government agency! He signed the other disclosures, gave Ryan his earnest money and pre-qualification letter, and the package was complete.

Ryan said he would send everything into HUD and they would have signed docs back from HUD in a few days. Then they would get everything rolling with his loan and the inspection. He was not officially under contract until HUD accepted and signed everything.

Mo was not looking forward to more waiting and more stress until this house was locked up. Of course, then he would still not own it yet, and there was a ton of work to do after the contract was accepted. He was realizing why a lot of people did not buy HUD homes or foreclosures. It was a tricky and stressful process.

He knew it would all be worth it once he got the keys to the house.

41

Trust with caution

Mo had another few days to wait until they heard from HUD. HUD wanted you to hurry on everything, but they took their time on their end getting things signed. Ryan said it would be at least three days until they got the signed documents back from HUD. Ryan also said that Mo did not have to wait around doing nothing—he could go talk to Josie, the lender he had gotten pre-qualified with.

Mo realized he had not talked to her at all about the HUD house. Ryan assured Mo that Josie knew how to do HUD deals, and it would not be an issue. Mo gave her a call and told her about the house. She said she could not do much to get the loan started until HUD signed the documents, but she would be happy to meet him and go over what he should expect.

Mo was also anxious to get the inspection scheduled but Ryan said there was no way he should do that before HUD signs everything. He could talk to a few inspectors to let them know he would need them soon but should not schedule anything yet.

Mo headed over to Josie's office one day after work to chat about the loan and the house. Josie greeted Mo with "nice work" and gave him a high five when he walked in the office.

Mo replied with a "thank you" and a big smile.

Josie did not like to mess around with small talk. She was busy and liked to get right to the point. She started with, "There should be no problem getting a loan on a HUD house with the FHA escrow. I have done a lot of these, and once you know how HUD works, it is all very simple. Some lenders get tripped up on them if they have never worked with HUD before, but that won't happen here." Josie stopped for a second, took a sip of her coffee, and continued, "Now, you have 45 days to get your loan, which is plenty of time. There are some things that could trip the deal up, but it probably won't be from the loan. The inspection is the biggest hurdle as HUD will not fix anything and they will not lower the price under any circumstances."

Mo was not sure that was true. He chimed in, "I thought the seller would make repairs if they were required by the lender?"

"Nope. That is what the FHA repair escrow is for, and HUD will not make any other repairs. That escrow can be a little tricky because we have to get a new appraisal and hope it is not vastly different from the appraisal HUD already got on the property," Josie said.

"What!? Why do we need a new appraisal if HUD already got one and that is what they are basing their escrow repairs on?

"Good question," Josie replied, "They used to allow the buyer to use that appraisal, but they changed the rules a few years ago. We will have to order an appraisal and hope the appraisal comes in at value with no more repairs...or just a few more repairs."

Josie sipped some more coffee and continued, "We need the value to come in for at least as much as you are buying it for. Otherwise, we have to base the loan on a lower amount, and you have to bring more cash to closing."

Mo interrupted her, "Let me guess. That is not a valid reason for HUD to lower the price either?"

Josie replied, "You are catching on quickly! I don't think the appraisal will come in low because this is a great price and a great deal. I also do not think the repairs should be an issue from what Ryan told me about the home. If there are a few more repairs, we can increase the escrow amount up to $5,500, but we cannot go over that amount or the FHA 203B loan won't work. We would have to go the FHA 203K loan, which can be a pain and more expensive."

"Yes, I have heard of that loan, and it seems like it could be a great loan for houses that need a lot of work, but it also sounds very complicated," Mo said.

"It is complicated and takes a while, so lets try to avoid that route," Josie responded. "There are a few things I want to mention to you that I tell everyone. Don't think I am singling you out, as this is my speech to every single buyer no matter how many homes they have purchased."

"Okay. No offense taken," Mo said matter-of-factually with a smile on his face

Josie continued, "You should qualify for this loan with no problems. Your credit is good. You have income. And, you have few debts unlike many people your age. You still have to be careful not to derail this process. I have some rules for buyers.

First, do not buy anything with credit. No cars, furniture, TVs, pool tables, etc. Nothing until you close on the house and get the keys.

Second, save your cash just in case something comes up like the appraisal comes in a little low or we have some extra expense that you were not planning on. Don't assume you will need exactly what we talked about.

And third, do not sign for any financial obligation except this loan. Do not cosign for an apartment, a house, or sublet an apartment. Do not apply for a credit card. Stay financially celibate until you buy this house!"

Mo was a little taken aback. She was serious about this stuff. He knew that he should not go out and buy a car, but he did not know about the other stuff. He told Josie he wouldn't buy anything at all, including McDonald's, until he bought this house.

Josie said, "There is something else I wanted to ask you. What type of loan do you want? A 30-year fixed rate?"

Mo said, "I guess so. I had not really thought about it much. I thought all loans were the same."

Josie was quick to reply, "Nope, not even close. There is a huge different in payments for a 15-year loan compared to a 30-year loan. There are pros and cons to both, but most people go with the 30-year option because the monthly payment is cheaper. An ARM or adjustable rate mortgage has a lower interest rate in the in the beginning of the loan, but it can increase later on. For now, I will assume you want a 30-year fixed rate mortgage, but do some research and let me know if you want something else."

They talked about a few more things, and Mo headed home. He could not do much more until they had the signed contract.

Mo was feeling extremely lucky to have found Ryan. He had read so many stories about agents who do not know what they are doing, especially when dealing with foreclosures. He also heard stories about lenders who do not know what they are doing either. Not only did Ryan know his stuff, but he had recommended Josie, who knew her stuff as well.

Something Mo had not thought about was the appraisal they would order on the property. Mo knew he had to do the inspection, and Josie told him the appraisal should be scheduled about the same time because utilities could be on for both the appraisal and the inspection. Josie knew the water could not be turned on for the appraisal, but the other utilities would be to ready to go.

Josie had mentioned something else about HUD that was very interesting. He was getting an FHA loan, and they did not care if the water was on because the repairs could be escrowed. However, no other loan could use that escrow. If a buyer was getting a conventional loan, they would not be able to turn the water on or use an escrow repair fund in most cases. That was one of the most common ways HUD contracts fell apart from the very beginning.

Mo knew that his next house most likely would not be a HUD home. He could only get one FHA mortgage at a time, and it would be tough to use a conventional mortgage on a HUD home unless it was in great shape. The other interesting thing he learned was that he was only allowed to buy a HUD home as an owner occupant once every two years. He could not legally buy another HUD home in one year anyway unless he bought it as an investor and put much more money down.

He knew he was lucky to have found this HUD house. Ryan had said there were very few foreclosures in the current market. HUD homes used to be for sale all over the place right after the housing crash, but now that things had recovered, HUD homes were few and far between.

Now, he just had to figure out what kind of loan he wanted!

42

Loans are complicated

Mo thought he knew a lot about real estate after all of the research he had done. However, as he got further and further into the house-buying process, he realized how much he did not know. He had not even thought about a 15- or 30-year loan and barely knew what an ARM loan was. He figured he should do some more research and try to decide what the best loan was for him. He could let Josie decide, but he would be breaking one of his core rules: don't let other people tell you the best investment strategies for yourself. He was fine learning from other people and getting their input, but he was the decision maker.

Mo looked up the advantages of using a 15- or 30-year mortgage. A lot of people seemed to think the 15-year option was the best choice. The 15-year loan had lower interest rates, you would pay it off faster, and you would save a ton of money on interest. That all seemed great to Mo, but one thing really bothered him—his payment!

If he got the 30-year loan, the payment would be $859, but with the 15-year mortgage, his payment would be $1,141 a month. That was a huge difference! He would be killing his cash flow. His gut told him this was not a wise thing to do. Mo did some more research.

Most of the articles he read talked about how much money a 15-year loan saved you, but there were a few that talked about the 30-year option being better. They mentioned a few advantages the 30-year loan had over the 15-year loan:

-A lower payment

-You could qualify for a more-expensive house

-You could always pay the 30-year loan off faster if you wanted

-You have a lower debt-to-income ratio with the 30-year loan

One article that Mo really liked related the loan options to rental properties. The one point the article kept making was that it is hard to get mortgages if your debt-to-income ration is too high. A 15-year loan increases that ratio and will make it very hard to get a second mortgage on a house if you want to buy multiple rentals. Mo was not sure how he was going to buy multiple rentals at this point, but he knew that was the end goal.

Something else the article mentioned was you paid less interest on a 15 year loan, but you are paying much more into that loan to get that savings. The savings is spread out over many years—it does not happen in one lump sum. On Mo's loan, he figured that he would pay more than $50,000 extra into the 15-year loan than the 30-year loan over 15 years because the payments were so much higher.

If he were to save that money, he could invest it into another rental or two. He had already learned the huge advantages of buying real estate, and he knew he wanted that 30-year loan, even if it had a slightly higher interest rate.

Now Mo wanted to learn about ARMs. He knew a little about them and vaguely remembered someone saying something about them being responsible for the last housing crisis. He did not want to be responsible for the next housing crisis by getting an ARM, but Mo thought he would at least learn about them.

The basics of an ARM are a fixed-rate period followed by a period where the rate can increase, or in some cases, decrease. The most common ARMs have 5- or 7-year fixed time periods, but there are also three year, ten year, and other options. The big advantage to an ARM was the interest rate in the beginning of the loan is lower than a 30-year or sometime even a 15-year fixed rate mortgage.

The rate could be 1/4 to 1/2 a percent lower, which would mean Mo could save $30 a month on his payment with an ARM. That did not seem like a lot of money, but it could add up over time. That would be $360 a year Mo would be saving on his mortgage payment.

The downside to an ARM was the rate could increase after that fixed rate period. It could go up a percent or two each year. Mo did not want to have a loan with a 8 or 10% interest rate when he could have had a fixed rate mortgage with a 5% interest rate.

Right, then Mo thought of something. He was not going to have his FHA mortgage that long, at least he did not plan to. The FHA mortgage came with mortgage insurance, and he would eventually want to get rid of that. It might take him a year or two, but he would want to refinance the property into a loan without mortgage insurance as soon as he could. If he were to get a 5-year ARM loan and refinance the loan before that five years was up, he would be ahead if he got the ARM loan.

Now he had a lot to think about. He definitely wanted the 30-year mortgage, but did he really want to get an ARM? Was that too risky? What if he could not or did not end up refinancing out of the FHA mortgage?

He decided that even though it made sense to get the ARM, he would stick with the 30-year fixed rate mortgage, at least on this house. Maybe he would be more adventurous in the future.

43

Is change worth it?

Mo had a hard time concentrating at work with everything going on. Luckily, he was still using his new and improved attitude to do well, and work was not that hard. He was enjoying his promotion and extra money he was making. He was still waiting for news from Ryan regarding when the signed documents would come back from HUD. He could not move forward on the the house until he had them.

Mo wanted to get the inspection and appraisal scheduled soon, and he was super nervous about both. He could not do anything until he had that signed contract.

While Mo waited for the contract, he called a couple of inspectors Ryan had recommended. He liked them both but decided to go with the one Ryan said was the most thorough. The guy's name was Evan, and he had been a home inspector for 11 years. The cost of the inspection would be about $400, which included a pressure test. One reason Mo wanted to use Evan was he could do a pressure test. The other inspector said that Mo would need to get a plumber to do the pressure test.

As soon as Mo got the signed contract back from HUD, he could set up the inspection, and Josie could set up the appraisal. For now, it was a giant waiting game, and he hated it. Part of him began to have doubts about the deal. Was this a sign that this was a bad house for him? Did HUD decide that they did not want to sell the house for this price anymore? Why was it taking so long!

He knew it had only been a few days, and Ryan told him it might take this long, but it was still agonizing.

He tried to distract himself by thinking about work and what he might really love to do. He still thought internet marketing would be a career he'd love. He really enjoyed real estate and thought he would love to be a full time investor at some point, but he didn't know how he could make a career of it yet.

Mo started to think about his job again. Even though he was doing much better, he knew it was not a long term solution. It was more of a stepping stone to his next big move and something he needed to buy his first house.

Since deciding that internet marketing might be the best career route for him, he had been reading and learning as much as he could about the subject, just like he had done with real estate. It was an extremely interesting subject, and that was a positive sign that it was something he should pursue. Mo had plenty of computer and internet skills. He also felt that he had marketing skills after noticing all the different marketing he was exposed to when learning about real estate.

The trick would be find a company or person who would be willing to hire him as an internet marketer, especially when he had no specific experience with marketing, although he did have experience with computers and the internet. Mo was very intrigued with this business as well because he knew there be a seamless transition from working for someone else into starting his own business. If he ever wanted to start on his own, it would take very little capital or startup money to create an internet marketing business.

His plan was to work for someone for a couple of years so he could gain experience. After he learned enough about the business, he could start his own internet marketing company.

It seemed crazy to think that he could have his own company in a year or two. Just a few weeks ago he was thinking it was insane how much money some people made who had their own companies. Then, it seemed insane to think about how much responsibility they had and stress they must go through. Now, Mo was thinking about starting his own company and was going through exactly what they were going through.

Mo knew that none of this would have be possible without the push he got from real estate. When he started this journey, it all seemed so foreign and far away. Now, he was really close to getting his first house. He had learned so much and realized that so much more was possible with his life if he wanted more to happen.

44

Share in the excitement

Mo finally heard from Ryan two days later, and Ryan gave him the good news that HUD had accepted his contract. Mo was officially under contract on a HUD home! They had 15 days to complete the inspection, and Mo wanted to try to schedule the appraisal the same time as the inspection.

Ryan said it would be best to schedule the inspection as far out as possible to give the appraiser time to schedule the appraisal. Ryan told Mo that it took some time to get the appraisal scheduled, and the later the inspection was, the better.

Mo scheduled the inspection for two weeks away, which would be the 14th day from when HUD signed the contract. He called Josie and told her the good news. Apparently, she had already known about it because Ryan texted her. She had gotten started on the loan and said she would request the appraisal for the same time period as when the inspection was being done.

Now, Mo had to wait two weeks! There was nothing he could do during that time real-estate wise. He was not sure how he would handle waiting that long for the inspection and appraisal. He had no choice but to wait, so he had to handle it some way.

Mo decided to talk Sarah and tell her all that had happened. He walked over to her desk and asked, "You have a few minutes to talk? Or, want to grab lunch?"

"Either one is fine with me," she replied. "What do you want to do?"

Mo had not talked with her for a while except for some chit chat here and there. He thought it would be nice to have some lunch and tell her everything that had been going on. "Lets grab some lunch."

30 minutes later, they walked to the same restaurant where they first had lunch.

They chatted on the way without talking about much of anything. Still, Mo enjoyed talking to Sarah and enjoyed being around her. She was smart, pleasant, and down to earth. They got to the restaurant, were seated immediately, and Mo decided not to wait to long to get into what he wanted to talk about.

"I got that HUD house officially under contract," he started.

"I was wondering what was going on with that deal," she said. "It had been so long that I thought maybe it had fallen through or you had second thoughts."

Mo replied, "I did not realize it, but it takes a long time to get a HUD house under contract. I was waiting forever, and now I have even more waiting to do. It will be two weeks before I can do my inspection or appraisal on the home."

"Two weeks is not that long in the grand scheme of things," Sarah said. "Not to mention—time goes by really fast, but it seems to slow down when we are waiting for really exciting things. While it might seem like a bad thing that you have to wait two weeks, maybe something really incredible will happen in that two weeks. Just enjoy the days you have and stop worrying so much. Plus, if time slows down, you won't age as fast."

Mo was not sure what to say to that. She had just twisted his world around with her philosophy on time. She was being very quirky and opening up more with him. That was a little unexpected from the normally cut-and-dry Sarah. He was not sure if she was saying that to make him feel better or if she really believed it. Either way, she had a point. He could waste the next two weeks worrying about things he could not change, or he could live his life and enjoy them.

Now, he had to decide what the best thing he could do with his time was. He could work on his new career. He could focus on his job. He could even hang out with his friends who he had not seen for months. They probably hated him by now, but maybe that was something he owed them. Or, maybe he was being cocky thinking they wanted to see him at all.

Either way, he had nothing to lose by seeing how Cory and Rob were doing without him. There was one more option that was creeping up in the back of his mind, but he decided to ignore that for now.

45

Old connections

It was tough, but Mo decided to text Rob. Rob and Cory had both tried to get Mo to hang out with them after Mo stopped going to the bars and getting drunk all the time. He was not mean to them. He didn't stand them up. He just slowly drifted away from that life. He was hoping that they would be cool and at least talk to him.

Mo sent the text. "Hey man. How's it going? Long time no talk. I was wondering if you guys wanted to hang out sometime."

Mo got a reply within about 10 seconds. "Holy Shit! You are alive? Of course we can hang out. You tell us when, and we will be there"

Mo and Rob hashed out the details and figured out they would all hang out at Rob's place that Saturday. They could figure out from there if they wanted to go out or not. Mo was excited. He knew he did not want to go back to the bar life, but it would be fun to hang out with those guys and relax for a bit.

Mo took it easy the next two days. He got all his work done and learned more about managing people, but he was not going crazy trying to add more chaos to his life. He thought he had enough going on with the house, and he felt like he had been learning and expanding non stop.

He was not done learning, but he thought he deserved a break.

Saturday came, and Mo found himself excited and nervous at the same time. It was a weird feeling. He had been so close with his friends only a short couple of months ago and now felt like he barely knew them. It was hard to comprehend how quickly everything had changed with him. It seemed like the world around him had stood still but Mo had jumped ahead a notch or two.

Mo still had plenty of books to read, and even though he said he would take it easy with all of the learning, he found himself reading Saturday afternoon in order to calm down a little bit. He was reading about "house hacking." It was a fascinating strategy that involved buying a multifamily property, which was a property with more than one unit. You live in one of the units and rent out the rest. It was a bit more complicated than what Mo was doing now, and he was intrigued by the strategy. Maybe he would house hack with the next house he bought.

It was time to head to Robs' place. On the way, he stopped by the liquor store and saw the giant 30 pack he used to always buy. He passed right by it and bought a 6 pack of some craft beer he had never heard of. Now, Rob and Cory would really think he had changed. Mo laughed out loud a little in the liquor store, and one of the other patrons gave him a sideways glance. He ignored them and paid for his lone six pack. He did not feel like getting hammered. He wanted to enjoy and remember the night.

Mo Parked in Rob's parking lot, walked up to his door, and knocked. Rob answered right away with Cory right behind him. They looked at each other for a second or two, and then Rob gave him a huge smile and hugged Mo. Mo could not help but smile and give both of them a hug back. They laughed and all walked over to the couch where they had previously spent hours, days, weeks, months, hanging out.

Mo set down his six pack of beer and waited for them to berate him for his choice of beverage. Cory reach over, grabbed one of the beers, and examined the bottle. He nodded and said, "Nice choice. We had some of this a few weeks ago."

Mo stared at Cory in disbelief. He had never seen Cory drink a craft beer in his life. He thought Cory had to be joking, but after a minute, it was clear he was not.

"Seriously?" Mo asked, "You two drink craft beer now? What the hell happened while I was gone?"

Rob replied, "Well, we both did a lot of talking and a lot of thinking when you left. We realized that we may be a little too old for our college lifestyle. Maybe we should be expanding our drinking habits a little."

Cory added to what Rob was saying, "Yeah, you kind of jogged us out of our funk we were in. We realized that we are not getting any younger, and maybe we all needed a change. It was almost a good thing when you left because we all took a look at our lives and realized we did not really like what we saw. I know you had tried to tell us that, but we would not listen when you were still hanging out at the end. I think you had to leave for us to notice."

"Wow," Mo said, "I had no idea you guys felt that way. I was expecting you to be doing the same things and getting mad at me for messing up the party. I guess I am not the only one who changed!"

The three of them talked for hours about Mo's adventures in real estate. They also talked about Rob and Cory's lives, which had changed as well. They all seemed to be progressing in life instead of living for the weekends. Mo was impressed the other two actually seemed to listen to him when he talked about real estate this time. They did not get hammered. They did not even go to the bar. They just hung out as friends and talked. It was really cool.

After a few hours of talking, they all decided to part ways. Mo headed home and had a really good feeling about how the night went. Rob and Cory had said they missed hanging out with him and he could come over anytime...even if he didn't bring beer!

46

Be bold

Mo had been lowkey at work and managed to relax for a few days. He had a great time with Rob and Cory but did not hang out with them again. He knew he could hang out with them once in a while, but he did not want to make it a regular thing and fall back into his old ways. They had said they had changed, but he knew how easy it would be for all of them to fall back.

His inspection was still a week away, and he was doing his best to keep himself occupied. That thing that had been in the back of his mind was Sarah. She seemed to be a boring accountant on the outside, but she was very interesting. She always kept Mo on his feet, had something interesting to say, and was very smart. She was also encouraging, and it seemed to be genuine.

Mo was still not sure if he could handle much more change in his life as the last few months seemed like a whirlwind. However, part of him was thinking he had managed this much change, why not try a little more. Mo decided to go for it. He was tired of being scared or lackadaisical. He was always just letting things happen instead of going for them. It had not worked out well in the past, and now that he was going for something, it was awesome. The real estate journey had made him a new person, added excitement, and gave him something to look forward to. He was no longer working for the weekend.

Mo was at work, and it was almost lunch time. He could walk over to Sarah's desk and ask her to lunch, but he had done that before, and that was the easy way out. They would talk and have a good time, but when it was over, they would get back to work and the lunch would be forgotten. He needed to be bold. He walked over to her desk.

She was typing away at her computer but looked up and stopped when she saw him walking towards her. She said, "Hey stranger. What brings you over this way? Looking for someone to take you to lunch?

Mo smiled at her then gave her a coy look and said, "Nope. I already have lunch plans. Sorry." He had no plans, but he had planned what he was going to say, "I had another question for you."

"What's that?" she asked, a curious tone to her voice.

Mo said, "Well you told me that time can go really fast and that this two weeks might fly by."

"I do remember saying that," she said, still with curiosity in her voice

Mo continued, "Well, time has not been going fast at all! It has been going incredibly slow. You also said that maybe something incredible will happen in these two weeks."

Sarah responded again, "I vaguely remember saying that too." She seemed to really be interested in what Mo was getting at now.

Mo kept talking, "Well nothing incredible has happened either. In fact, it has been an extremely boring and uneventful period in my life. However, today I decided to change that. I decided that it was time to stop waiting for something incredible and to make it happen. So...have dinner with me this Friday night."

Sarah looked at him with an amused face. Mo was beginning to think this was a huge mistake and she was going to start laughing, possibly historically, in the middle of the office.

She looked at him straight in the eyes and said, "I am glad you specified Friday night because I hate having dinner in the morning or the middle of the day. Plus, I have to work."

Mo was pretty sure she was making fun of him, but his mind was racing, and he was not quite sure. Had he said something stupid? He couldn't really remember exactly what he had said. Doesn't she know it is not an easy thing to ask a girl out for the first time! He said the smartest thing he could thing of. "I generally like to have dinner at night as well."

Sarah started laughing, but not hysterically. Mo felt a sense of relief, as it was a hearty happy laugh that meant she was having a good time. It was not a nervous twitchy laugh that meant she was trying to figure out how to reject him in a nice way. Or, maybe she was a super bitch and her favorite thing to do was embarrass people who asked her out. She stopped laughing but had a big smile on her face and said, "I am sorry for making a joke out of this, and I would love to have dinner with you. You are by far the coolest and most exciting guy around here, which says a lot! I would be lucky to enjoy some more time outside the office besides our occasional lunches."

Mo felt a wave of relief as soon as she said she would love to go out with him. He had a pretty good hunch she would say yes, but you never knew with these things. He knew she was being partially sarcastic, which he really liked, and he had done what she said would happen.

He had created something incredible...or at least dinner.

47

Don't be nervous

Friday night came, and Mo was ready. He had prepared for his date with Sarah. He had come to the conclusion that he needed to treat every aspect of his life the same way that he was treating real estate. In the past, he would have let everything come to him. If it worked out, great. If it did not, it must not have been meant to be. He was realizing that things tend to work out a lot better if you put in the work to make them work out.

He cleaned his car and apartment. He shaved and showered out and spent some time figuring out something to wear that did not look too stupid. He even bought her flowers. He was ready to go. He was supposed to pick her up at her place, and they were going to figure out on the fly where to eat. He had a few places in mind, but he thought it was kind of fun that she wanted to be spontaneous and not plan everything.

Mo got to her place, which was only a couple of miles from his apartment. He did a once over in the mirror, got out of the car, and walked up to her building. He figured out where her unit was in the complex, which was giant, and headed that direction.

He got to her door and felt some nerves, but what was he going to do?

Go home? He knocked on the door, and someone else answered it right away. Not just someone else, but a guy! Mo was not expecting this and had a hard time saying anything when the guy gave him a rough, "Can I help you?"

"Uhh, yeah. I am...umm...is Sarah here?" Mo stammered

The guy said, "Yeah, she is here, but who wants to know?" In a very unfriendly way. He looked at Mo like he was going to punch him, but before Mo could say anything, he started laughing and patted Mo on the shoulder. He managed to say in between laughs, "I am sorry, man. I am just giving you a hard time. I am Sarah's brother. Come in, and she will be right out."

Mo was still not sure what to say. He was holding the flowers still and felt a little dorky. He walked in and sat on the couch that her brother pointed to. The apartment was not huge, but it was clean and efficient. It definitely looked like a woman's place, and Mo guessed her brother was either visiting or some kind of short-term roommate. Her brother sat on the couch next to Mo. Mo said, "I'm Mo," and he put his hand out for a handshake "I was not expecting you. You got me pretty good there."

Her brother said, "I am sorry...that was not very nice of me. I'm Chris." He shook Mo's hand. "Sarah is letting me stay here for a little bit while I get some things in order. She is a sweetheart."

Mo was still at a loss for words but managed to squeak a few things out, "Sarah is great. We have worked together for a while, and she has always been one of my favorite co-workers." Mo thought that had sounded super lame, but he was not here to impress her brother, or maybe he was. Who knows what was going on. Finally, Sarah walked through a hallway, and Mo felt a sense of relief. He said, "Hey! I was just getting to know your brother."

She replied, "Don't get too comfortable. Let's get out of here' I am starving!"

Mo got up, and they walked out the door. Once outside the hallway, he gave her the flowers and said, "These are for you."

She said, "Thank you. I was hoping they were for me and not for my brother...or that my brother did not give you flowers. That would be a little weird."

Mo knew Sarah was sarcastic, but it was getting worse as he got to know her more. Or maybe it was getting better. He was a huge fan of sarcasm. However, his nervousness and encounter with Chris had left him with no witty comebacks. All he could say was, "No, I bought them, and they are definitely for you." She smiled and smelled the flowers as they walked to the car. Mo decided to be honest, "Your brother threw me off back there. I mean, he really messed with my head. So, sorry if I am a bit quiet as I try to figure out what the hell just happened."

Sarah threw here head back and laughed. Then, she looked at Mo and said, "I am so sorry. My brother is a complete a-hole sometimes, but he is also really funny. He asked if he could mess with you some, and I told him that would be awesome. We can see what you are made of."

Mo looked at her with a fake I-am-pissed-off face and said, "You! You gave him permission to do that? Do you have any idea what goes through a guy's head when he is getting ready to knock on the door of a girl he is going out with for the first time? We already are working with a quarter of our normal brain cells, and you agreed to let him mess with me?"

"Yup," she said. "Like I said, I wanted to see how you reacted. You did well. We knew there was a small chance you might go berserk and attack him, but I was willing to take that chance."

Mo said, "What if I would have just left?"

Sarah said, "If you would have given up that easy, then the test would have been well worth it. I don't need guys who run away from everything."

They got to Mo's car, and he opened the passenger door for her. He realized she had never seen his car before. They had always walked to lunch. She looked it over, got inside, and peaked around the interior. She said, "This is nice. Not too fancy. It is clean. You seem to have made a responsible decision buying this vehicle."

Mo looked at her with fake shock and said, "What do you mean not too fancy? What are you expecting, a Rolls Royce?"

Sarah laughed again, which she did a lot, and said, "I mean that...well...some guys in your position and stage in life will spend all their money on their car. They make $40,000 or $50,000 a year and buy a brand new BMW or Mercedes. They can't really afford the car, but they are too concerned with looking cool to let that stop them. This is a nice car, but it is not brand new yet still unique and a step above boring."

Mo was back to his in-shock phase and was not sure what to say. Most girls he had went out with in the past would not say as many interesting things in the entire night as Sarah had said in the first five minutes. He looked at her with newfound respect and said, "I am glad you like the car. I do too, but I have no idea where we are going. I have a few places in mind, unless you were set on somewhere."

Sarah looked at him and said, "I know exactly where we are going. Drive south, and I will tell you how to get there. You do know which way south is, right?"

Mo laughed this time and said, "Yes, I know which way south is." He pulled out of the parking space and headed straight north.

They both laughed and had a wonderful rest of the night.

48

Inspection day

Mo had made it to inspection day. He had been mellow at work and managed to relax for a few days. He had a great date with Sarah, and they had hung out a few more times while he was waiting for the inspection. When he thought about it that way, he knew he was not being fair to her. She was not something to keep him occupied until his inspection came. He liked her and had a great time whenever he was with her. Even if he was not buying a house, he would still be happy to hang out with her. The bonus was that she was really supportive of his initiative and drive to buy a house.

He was so much happier because he was taking control of his life, even though he had not technically bought a house yet. He had gotten a promotion and felt like he had been enlightened by his new attitude the last few months.

The inspection was today and the appraisal tomorrow. The inspector Mo hired was recommended by Ryan. Ryan had explained that an inspector can make or break a deal. Some inspectors will look for any minor defect and try to make it sound like a big deal to justify their cost and job. Other inspectors can be lackadaisical and fail to inspect the entire house. Ryan said they needed an inspector who was in the middle and would inspect the entire property, find all the issues, but also let Mo know what was a big deal and what was minor problem.

Ryan said something else that really surprised Mo. Ryan told Mo that inspectors did not have to be licensed or have any training at all. Mo could be an inspector today if he wanted. Buyers have to be very careful about the inspectors they choose and make sure they know what they are doing. There are also no guarantees that an inspector will find everything that is wrong with a house. They can't tear into the walls, so there is a chance they could miss some things.

Mo and Ryan met the inspector at 10:00 a.m. Mo used one of his vacation days. The inspector's name was was Rich, and he appeared to be in his 50s. Mo realized he was not very good at telling how old people were once someone was over 30. Rich had a little truck with a ladder and a bunch of tools.

Ryan introduced them and said he would be back in a couple of hours. Ryan did not have time to be at the entire inspection, and Mo was fine with that. However, Mo was planning to stay, bug Rich as much as he could, and learn as much as he could.

Rich would look for anything that is wrong with the home. However, he was not going to dig into the walls, fish out wires, or look for long-lost pottery in the house. Rich told Mo it was actually easier to inspect a house with an unfinished basement because you could see so much more than when the walls are covered with sheet rock. Rich was very clear in saying that he might not see everything was wrong with a home, but he would do the best he could just as Ryan had said.

Rich said some inspectors do offer a guarantee. However, the price would be triple. Mo's inspection was $400, and he felt like he did not need to spend an extra $800 for a guarantee that really was no guarantee at all since it only protected Mo against things the inspector could see and inspect.

Rich told Mo that he can find something wrong in every house, whether it is 100 years old or brand new. He has found houses that were completely remodeled with major structural problems, and he has seen houses that looked like they were about to fall down but actually were not nearly as bad as they appeared.

Mo followed Rich around the house and looked at everything as closely as he could. Rich looked at the roof, but Mo was not allowed to follow him up the ladder due to liability reasons. Rich checked out the electrical system, the plumbing, the HVAC, the appliances, the foundation, and many more things that Mo lost track of.

Rich could see some of the concrete walls in the basement laundry room. There were some cracks in the walls that worried Mo, but Rich did not seem to worry about them. Rich was quick to say that Mo should bring in an expert for more inspections on anything he was worried about, but then Rich would also explain his thought process. Rich told Mo that the cracks were nothing to worry about. Cracks that were more than a 1/4 inch wide or cracks where one side stuck out more than 1/4 inch from the other side were something to worry about. Even those cracks would probably be fine, but if the cracks got to be more than a 1/2 inch apart, you really need to have them inspected by an engineer. These cracks were tiny, and Rich said they were very common in most houses.

Rich said the roof looked fine but that many times hail damage cannot be seen by the naked eye from the ground. You had to get up on the roof and either be experienced at looking for hail damage or get a roofer to see what condition the roof is actually in. Rich said you could tell right away if there were problems with some roofs as the shingles would be peeling away from the surface. That was a sure sign the roof needed to be replaced. Rich also said it was a very bad sign if there was more than one layer of shingles on a roof. The more layers of shingles a roof has, the shorter the lifespan of that roof. Most lenders and insurance companies will not accept a roof that has multiple layers. Code used to allow up to three layers of shingles on a roof, but that changed to only allow one. Rich told Mo they would talk more about code violations later.

Rich said the furnace looked okay but was about 10 years old. He said that most furnaces should last up to 30 years, but many fail before that due to a lack of maintenance. A furnace should be cleaned and inspected every year. The furnace filters should be changed every couple of months. He thought the furnace should last many more years but that it would not hurt to have an HVAC company come take a look at it to be sure.

Rich could see some of the piping in the laundry room in the basement. He said that most homes this age have copper pipes, but sometimes a house this old would have galvanized pipes. Rich said that galvanized pipes almost always need to be replaced eventually. They would rust from the inside, reducing water flow and contaminate the water. Copper pipes are great and last many years, as does pex piping, which is plastic. This property happens to have copper pipes, which Rich was very happy about.

The tricky part with this house was Rich and Mo knew the home had broken pipes somewhere. However, they could not turn the water on to see where the break was. Rich brought an air compressor with him and said they would do an air test to see if they could pinpoint where the leak is. He could send air through the system, and hopefully, they could hear where the air was leaking.

Rich hooked up the air compressor, made sure all the faucets were off, and turned it on. The air compressor hissed away as it sent air through the entire plumbing system. Mo and Rich were in the basement and could hear the air leaking out of the system almost immediately. Rich walked around the laundry room and found a small break in a pipe where the washing machine water supply was. It looked like someone had twisted the pipe trying to get the hose off and crinkled it, causing it to crack. They walked around the rest of the house and could not hear or see any other problems. Rich said he hoped that was it because it was a simple fix.

Rich said the electrical seemed to be in decent shape. He cautioned to have electrician look at it to make sure. Rich said again that an inspector was someone who knew a fair amount about many different subjects but are not an expert in every single thing. Rich did say to watch out for knob-and-tube wiring and fuses and many wires taped together.

Rich also told Mo about the sewer line and how it is smart to get it scoped. He had not scheduled the scope but said he could do it for an extra charge. He said sometimes the sewer line on older houses is made of clay and can have cracks or breaks in it. Rich said that most sewer lines will last quite a while, even with cracks or breaks, but many people worry about them. Rich told Mo that most people do not get the scope because of the extra charge, but it could find a major problem. It was rare, but in some cases, a bad sewer line could cause the sewer to back up into the home. Replacing a sewer line could cost from $5,000 to $25,000 depending on the age and size of the line.

Mo was tight on his budget, and while he thought maybe he should be getting the line scoped, he decided not to.

Another issue that Rich brought up was Radon. Radon is a gas that was shown to cause cancer in certain studies. Radon is odorless and invisible, but it naturally occurs in some areas of the country. Basements are especially susceptible to it. Rich said he can do a test for Radon and highly suggested that test because most sellers are willing to make some repairs when the Radon is high. Mo reminded Rich this was a HUD home, and HUD did not make repairs. Rich smiled and said he almost forgot about that. Rich said if the results are too high, a Radon system could be added to the property, and it would cost from $1,000 to $1,500.

Rich also looked at some other items that were not to current code. He said that code constantly changes over the years depending on when a house is built. A house may be up to code for when it was built but not up to the current codes. Usually, if a house is older than 10 years, something is not going to be to code. That doesn't mean the house is not safe to live in, just that it is not built up to the current standards. Some of those standards are important to pay attention to, and others are not as important.

On this house, the were many things that were not to current code because it was an older house. To get the house to current codes, you would have to rebuild it, which was not a feasible option. Rich said he tried not to worry about what was up to code and what was not up to code. Another problem with codes is that every city has different codes, and it is impossible for him to know every requirement. He likes to look at if a house is safe, not if it is up to all the current codes.

Ryan came back for the last half hour or so of the inspection. Ryan and Mo talked about what Rich had found up to that point. The biggest issue with the home was the furnace being a little older and that they cannot tell exactly how good of shape it is in. Rich had suggested Mo have an HVAC company come look at the furnace and see exactly what condition it was in. The other issue that Rich found was there were no GFCIs (special electrical outlets) installed in the bathrooms and kitchen. Current code suggested all bathrooms and kitchens have GFCI outlets, but Rich said installing them wasn't very expensive. They can prevent a fire or other problems with the electrical system.

Mo knew with his inspection that you can either accept the house as it is or cancel the contract. He had no choice of asking the seller to make any repairs or give any credit. HUD was very clear that you took the house as it was, or someone else would take the house as it was.

Mo had a few worries about the furnace and maybe electrical system, but he decided it was worth the chance. He may get the sewer line scoped at some point, and he would get the Radon checked, but he was not going to let those items stop him from buying the house. He should also probably have an HVAC company come check out the furnace to make sure it is safe. But, he was not going to let that kill the deal.

Mo thanked Rich and Ryan for helping get closer to buying his first ever house. The inspection had gone better than he thought it would. There were some minor problems, but he knew he was getting a good enough deal that he could handle everything.

Mo was one step closer to buying his first home!

49

What is an appraisal?

Mo was not out of the woods yet, as the appraisal still had to be completed. The appraiser was coming the day after the inspection.

The appraiser was hired by the lender, and their job is to verify the value of a property. The bank is lending Mo money on a property that is being bought for $118,000 and some change. The lender wants to make sure the house is really worth that if they're lending money to Mo. The appraiser is not supposed to come up with the exact amount of what the house should be worth. The appraiser is supposed to confirm the house is or is not worth as much as the bank is lending. The appraiser will attach a value to the home, but that value is not always what people think it is.

Ryan told Mo not to expect the appraisal to come in much higher than the contract price. Mo was a little surprised since he thought the appraisal was meant to tell him what the house was worth. Ryan told Mo that even if the house was worth $200,000, the appraisal might come in at $119,000. The appraiser is under pressure not to come in at a high price. There was a lot of mortgage fraud before the last housing crisis, and much of the fraud came from fake or elevated appraisals. The appraisal system was changed to counter that fraud.

Many appraisers will not come in much higher than the contract price because they do not want to draw attention to themselves with a high appraisal.

Ryan told Mo that he also saw appraisals come in lower than the contract price in some cases for the same reasons. Ryan said that just like any profession, there are good and bad appraisers. Most appraisers do an amazing job and try to value a property fairly. While there are some appraisers who tend to come in low on everything and think they are doing the banks or buyers a favor by doing so, in reality, a low appraisal usually costs the buyer money and has a good chance of killing the deal.

This had Mo little bit worried because he really did not want the appraisal to mess up his deal. Ryan said the appraisal should not have an effect on this property because it was such a good deal, and from what everyone can see, the repairs really were pretty minor. He also said that if house were completely fixed up and was under contract for more money than any other house in the neighborhood, that would worry him. He was not worried about this appraisal because the price was so good.

Mo also asked if there was anything they could do to help the appraiser out. Ryan had said that they do often help the appraisers out, but they have to be careful because they don't want to appear to be influencing the appraisers value. Ryan said he can pull up recently sold comparable properties in the same neighborhood to show that the house is worth at least as much as it is under contract for. They can send those properties to the appraiser, and they can also mention any repairs or qualities of the property that may not be visible.

Ryan was clear that this property did not have a lot of really great qualities that could not be seen. However, he would still send a list of comparable sold properties, and if Mo was ever trying to sell a house that he had just fixed up, that was when it was important to list all the repairs that had been done.

Ryan also told Mo that it was best if they did not show up at the appraisal. Most appraisers wanted to look at the house on their own and not be bothered. Mo really wanted to go to see how it was done and talk to the appraiser, but Ryan convinced him to stay away. They would have to wait for the inspection and the appraisal report which could take a few days or even a week to come back with a value.

Mo would have to be patient again!

50

Things need to change

M o went back to work the next day while the appraisal was being done. He was tempted to head over to the house to meet the appraiser, even thought Ryan had told him not to. He controlled himself and stayed at work.

Work was still okay. He liked the people there more since he let himself get to know them. He had not formed any deep relationships with anyone but was getting to know people better and better. His new management position was not much different than what he did before he was a manager. He was able to guide the IT department (all three of them) a little more but mostly the did the same stuff they did before he became the manager. He was supposed to be getting some training on how to manage people, but he had not seen much of that yet.

Tory had been busy with his management position, and he told Mo that they did not have anyone available to train him. Mo was on his own, but again, it was not like he had a whole lot more to do.

Mo was really excited and motivated when he had gotten the promotion and talked to Tory a month or two ago. That excitement was wearing off quickly, especially since he had made so much progress with the HUD house. He thought maybe he could keep working at his job for a while longer since he was moving up the corporate ladder. However, he was not sure how much higher he could move up based on the tiny IT department and the lack of attention that department received. Mo was beginning to wonder if the promotion was simply a way to keep Mo working there with no intention of letting him get too far up in the company.

That left Mo with a couple of options. He had time to think, as he could not do anything with the house until the appraisal came in. Actually. he could not do much at all. even when the appraisal came in. It was all up to other people when and how the process worked. He had to depend on the appraiser to come in at value with no more or at least minimal additional repairs. He had to rely on his lender to get that appraisal and proceed with the loan process. He had to depend on Ryan to get everything else in order for him to purchase the home.

He was antsy, excited, nervous, frustrated, and overall full of energy that he did not know what to do with. He could not do anything with the house but wait. He could not do much at work, except for that project that he was less than excited about—the one to improve their IT systems . He had hinted to Tory about improving things a few times, and Tory was less than enthusiastic about changing anything. Tory had told Mo that things seemed to work just fine, and he saw no reason to spend money or resources on something that was not broken.

That left Mo with few options. He decided he needed to take a look at his career options and figure out what to do with his life. His current job was not going to work for him much longer.

51

A new career?

o decided to approach his new career like he did real estate. He would research as much as he could about possible paths and not take the process lightly. He had taken most of his life lightly up to this point and realized how much he had let fate and other outside factors affect him. He had basically floated to where he was now. He always took the path of least resistance.

The path of least resistance is not the best way to get where you want to go. In fact, many times it will take you the opposite direction of where you want to go. Mo was not too far off from what he really wanted in life, but he knew he had to change things if he wanted to live life to its fullest.

Mo purchased books on starting a business and internet marketing. While he was waiting for those books, he did as much research as he could online. Mo was bombarded by internet marketing sites selling training and education. He could not believe how hard it was to find any actual information. He thought real estate had a lot of marketing going on, but this was crazy.

There were so many sites and so many opinions on the best practices for what he wanted to do. He knew a lot about the internet side and the computer side of the business, but he did not know much about the marketing side. He was getting a little worried about his chosen profession. How was he going to navigate this business, find a job in this business, or start his own business with so much competition?

It seemed he would have to learn about search engine optimization (SEO), social media marketing, email funnels, landing pages, copy writing, and content creation, and that was just the beginning. It was overwhelming, and he had no idea where to start.

Then he thought about something. He had felt the exact same way when he started looking into real estate. He had no idea what he was doing. In fact, he knew less about real estate than he knew about internet marketing. At least he was already in the computer industry. He was able to learn about real estate and navigate through all the marketing, and he had almost bought a house from that education within a few short months.

What had drawn him to the internet marketing career was the various marketing techniques he had seen companies use when he was researching real estate. He thought he would take the same approach he did with real estate. He would research the broad idea of internet marketing then narrow down his research to specific niches in the industry. He would figure out which niche he thought suited him best, and he would focus on that.

He had a lot of work ahead of him, but he knew it would not be easy when he started this journey. He still had no clue how he would make a business of this or how he would even find a job that involved what he wanted to do. He also had no idea how he would buy a house when he started getting interested in real estate. He figured that meant he was on the right track!

52

Could he start a businsess?

I t had been a few more days, and Mo had not heard back from Ryan on the appraisal. He knew it might take a while, but Mo was hoping that the appraisal would come in sooner rather than later.

Mo had been busy reading as much as he could about his possible new career. He learned that it was a very competitive field, but there was also a ton of demand for marketing. Everyone was online, and most everyone wanted to market themselves online in one way or another. Mo was worried about the competition at first, but he was less worried now that he realized how internet marketing could be used for every profession and every business.

Mo had read about websites, blogs, products, and a lot of other aspects of marketing in the online world. Even though Mo loved computers and technology, he was realizing how little he knew about online marketing and how little he had learned in school about it. They taught him almost nothing about marketing in school. He had learned how to program—and a lot about technology—but he had not learned how to make money with it. He had been programmed to work for someone else at a job. He had learned how to do specific tasks and let someone else (his boss) worry about how those tasks translated into creating value.

Mo was worried about the business aspect of everything, but he was not focused on that side of it now. He wanted to learn what part of the business he would focus on and then learn about the business side of everything. If he was lucky, maybe he could find a job or create a job where he could put those skills to use while he learned how to run a business or start one.

He did not want to overwhelm his brain with too many things at once. He had learned that forcing himself to learn 20 different subjects at once did not work well. He tried that with real estate and got nowhere. He was better off learning one thing at a time until he understood that concept than trying to do it all at once.

Mo was still having a hard time narrowing down what he wanted to focus on. There was so much to learn and so many things to research. Everyone wanted to sell him on a program that would teach him how to sell things with social media, email, websites, and even cold calling!

Mo decided to look back at what attracted him to the websites he liked when learning about real estate. They were not pushy, and they offered real information he could learn right then, all without buying a high-priced program to learn all the secrets. He also wondered how they made any money with that model. He decided to check out some of the sites to see if he could figure it out.

He went to a few sites that taught him the most, and they used a blog style. It was basically an article written by the author of the site and sometimes a guest author. In some cases, Mo would read articles on big sites about real estate, but they tended to have much fewer details than the blogs. He loved seeing how certain blogs would have case studies on how to buy properties, how much money they would make, and how to finance the houses.

After peeking around the blogs for a while, he would see links to other programs or books, and Mo realized the site was making money by sending people to those sites. He also saw some advertisements on the sites that were sure to make money. Some of the blogs had their own coaching programs, which were money makers as well.

Almost every blog also offered some type of free gift to get people to sign up for their email list. Once on the list, Mo was sure they would try to sell people more products or coaching. Mo had seen much of this when he was learning about real estate, but he had not signed up for anything since the bad experience with Rich Dad Poor Dad coaching. Mo liked the blog style of marketing. You were providing useful information for people while making money. Mo could also see how it might be fun to write about his experiences and life, although it would be a bit scary as well. He was not sure he wanted the world to know how much he did not know.

Mo saw that most of the popular blogs also had a massive social media presence with Facebook, Twitter, Instagram, and other sites. A lot of the blogs cross promoted themselves with YouTube and other media outlets as well. Mo was intrigued, but again, he had no idea how much money these sites were making, and he imagined it would take years to make a significant amount of income from a blog.

He figured that writing a blog would offer more benefits than just making money. He could chronicle his journey, get feedback from others, and keep himself accountable since he was telling the world his plans.

53

It's never as bad as we imagine

Something else that Mo noticed while he was researching and figuring out what he wanted to do with his life was how much he still had to learn about real estate. He had learned a lot, but since he had written the offer and got it accepted by HUD, he had stopped reading real estate articles. He also had some books to read that he never finished.

He thought getting over the hump of buying your first house was a huge step, but he had not come close to learning everything he needed to learn to be a successful real estate investor. When he was reading the real estate blogs to learn about their marketing techniques, he also stumbled upon a lot of real estate techniques that he had never learned.

He had really only learned about rental properties—and only scratched the surface with them. There was so much more that he had wanted to learn when he first started this journey. In fact, the first training he was going to go to was about house flipping. It was not even about rental properties.

Mo's brain was awash with information, doubt, and questions. What were his next steps? Should he be learning about real estate or his career? Could he do both? Was he jumping into buying a house too soon without fully knowing what he was doing?

Mo paused for a minute or two and tried to make sense of his crazy life the last three months. Everything he had done with real estate, his job, and his career had been brand new. He was even starting a relationship. What if he was doing all this wrong and setting himself up for a huge disaster!

Mo felt a little panic swelling up in his stomach but forced himself to take some deep breaths. He tried to recall some of the things he had learned about his attitude and success. One thing popped into his head that had resonated with him was even if he lost everything, he still had his knowledge. No one can take that away from him.

He remember reading an article or book that talked about a writer who was almost finished with a book. He wrote the book on a typewriter, and his house caught on fire. The entire book was lost and months of work was gone. The writer had no backup, and people were horrified when they learned how he had lost the book.

People asked the writer, "What will you do now that you lost your entire book and have to start over?"

The writer replied, "I have not lost the book. I still have the book right here," and he pointed to his head. He added, "I may not have the book down on paper, but I know exactly what happens, when it happens, and how it happens. It will be more work writing the book again, but I have not lost anything."

The story was also related to other professions or even billionaires who had gone bankrupt before they made it big. The point was that when we are constantly learning and expanding, losing money is not a big deal. You can learn how to make more money and how to buy more things, but you do not lose the knowledge you have amassed over the years. Knowledge and knowing how to be successful is much more important than money.

First off, Mo told himself that he had not lost anything yet or screwed anything up either. He had not even bought the house. He had gotten a promotion, and he had learned how to expand his knowledge, which were all things that were big wins for him.

Secondly, Mo was excited with life! It may seem like he was being boring by not going out all the time, but he was having so much more fun learning. He was so much more excited about his future. He did not feel like crap and full of regret after a night of partying. Every day, he was improving his life and learning something new.

Mo immediately felt better and stopped panicking. He knew he was on the right track. Even if this house did not work out or he did not figure out the perfect career right now, things were getting better for him. He had to just keep moving and keep learning.

Mo decided it was time to take a break for the night and get some sleep. He still had to be to work on time, and he still needed his job to get this house.

54

Is this really happening?

The next, day Mo was at work talking to his co-workers (or underlings—he was not sure what to call the people who he managed). He was telling them it was okay to smile once in a while or engage in chit chat with the other employees. They never talked, and people always made comments about how anti social they were in the office. Mo thought that now that he was the manager, that negative feeling towards the IT department may make him look bad. He was trying to work on their people skills when he got a text from Ryan.

"Hey Mo. We got the appraisal back, and everything looks great! Give me a call when you get a chance."

Mo was ecstatic. He knew this was basically the last hurdle to buying the house, and at this point, he was dead set on buying this house. He excused himself from his little meeting and gave Ryan a call.

Mo and Ryan talked for a few minutes about the appraisal. Ryan said it came in right at $119,000, and the appraiser had actually asked for fewer items to be fixed than the HUD appraiser. The appraisal said that the plumbing still had to be repaired, but that was it. Even though there was some peeling paint on the trim of the outside of the house, the appraiser didn't say it needed to be repaired. Ryan said Mo could lower the repair escrow and would only have to worry about the plumbing leaks.

Ryan and Mo talked about the next steps for buying the house. Basically, there was not much for Mo to do except lay low. That meant not buying anything expensive, not getting a credit card, not buying any furniture, etc. Mo said he could handle all of that.

Ryan congratulated Mo and told him he just had to be patient for the loan to get approved now.

After talking to Ryan, Mo called his lender, Josie. He had not talked to her for a while, mostly because she and Ryan both told him that he did not need to talk to her. Now that the appraisal was in, he wanted to make sure there was nothing else he needed to do.

She answered right away, and they had a quick conversation about what would happen next. Josie told Mo that the underwriters would look over the appraisal and all of Mo's information. The underwriter was the person who actually approved the loan and made the final decisions. She told Mo not to worry as she rarely had problems with underwriting as long as she did her job well. She said that Mo was not pushing the debt-to-income ratios or credit score parameters, and it should be just fine. They just had to wait for that underwriter process to finish, which could take a week or two.

Mo also learned that the entire loan should be ready to go in about 30 days from when he got the signed contract back from HUD. Mo thought he had 45 days to close, so that was a surprise. Josie said he did not have to close in 30 days if he did not want to, but he could close early.

Josie added that the closing timeline might depend on when his lease ended for his apartment. Mo was a little in shock when she said that. Ryan had mentioned in the beginning of this whole process that Mo would have to deal with his apartment lease, but he had forgotten all about it! He had never checked to see when his lease was up! He did not need to be making lease payments while he owned the house.

Mo called the property management company as soon as he was done talking with Josie. He could not believe he had forgotten this step! He was able to reach the company right away, and after telling them who he was and where he lived, he was able to get some info out of them.

The lady on the line figured out who he was and said, "Okay Mo, I see you in our system now. What was it you were looking for?

Mo said a little nervously, "I wanted to know when my lease was up because I am thinking of buying a house." He did not want to tell her he was buying a house in a couple of weeks for some reason.

She said, "Well we have actually been meaning to call you. Your lease term was up this month, and we wanted to see if you were ready to sign a renewal again for one more year."

"Oh thank God!" Mo said. He quickly apologized. "I am sorry. I thought I had much more than that remaining on the lease. I actually do not want to renew for another year right now. What happens in that case?"

"Well, your lease will go to a month-to-month term, and you have to give us 30 days notice if you want to move out. We also have to give you 30 days notice if we want you to move out or if we decide to raise rents.

Mo thought about everything and said, "I would like to give my 30 days notice today then."

"We will need an email or something in writing saying that." She gave him the email address to send the notice to.

Mo had just burned one of his bridges. He no longer had a place to live in 30 days, so he had to buy the house now!

He had to share all of this with someone besides the people who were getting paid to help him out. He headed over to Sarah's desk. They had been taking things slowly, and she was by no means his girlfriend, but it was a strong possibility that would happen soon if things kept going they way they had been.

She was at her desk working away as she normally did. She smiled when she saw him coming and stopped what she was doing so she could give him her full attention. Then she said, "Well you look happy. What have you been up to?"

Mo said, "The appraisal came back okay, the inspection is good, and closing is set. I even terminated my lease on my apartment. I will soon be a new homeowner!"

Sarah smiled even more and gave him a high-five. "That is awesome!"

They talked a little longer about the timing, and Mo headed back to his desk. He could not stop from smiling at everyone he saw on the way.

55

Another path?

Mo decided to push out the closing as far as he could because it was the smartest financial decision. It was not easy to wait, but he had to pay rent for the next 30 days, and the longer he could put off buying the house, the less time he would be paying rent for his apartment and paying a mortgage.

The timing had worked out almost perfectly. He would be able to buy the house just a couple of days before his lease was up at the apartment. He would have time to move everything over to the house and clean the apartment without being in a huge hurry.

Ryan had mentioned that many people have to buy and sell their homes at the same time on the same day. They will put their house up for sale, get a contract on it, then try to find a house to buy and time the closings to happen on the same day. Ryan said it was super stressful and not the most fun thing to move all your stuff in one day. That was for people who already lived in a house and had accumulated a lot more things than Mo had.

Mo hoped that he could put himself in a good enough financial position that he would never have to buy a house and sell another on the same day. He had a long time to wait for that day as he had to live in the HUD home for at least one year, and he wasn't planning on selling it after that year. He was planning on renting it out and holding onto it for a very long time.

Mo was not sure what to do with his time. He had a long time to wait for the closing. He wanted to learn as much as he could about marketing and about real estate. He still felt lost in the marketing world because there was so much going on and so much he could do. He found himself daydreaming and not paying attention every time he tried to read or research marketing. When he learned about real estate, it had his full attention, and he rarely thought about anything else. He was starting to wonder if he should stick with his job and focus on real estate for now.

He had been telling himself he could not do much with real estate after he bought this house because he could not rent it out for at least one year. However, while he was doing all his research into his possible new career, he had been learning more about real estate. Yes, he probably could not buy many more rentals for a while after buying this house. He could not get another low-down-payment loan, and there was no way he had the 20 or 25% down he would need to buy a straight-up investment property.

While he could not buy another rental property, he could invest in real estate in other ways. There was flipping, which was very interesting, but also very hard from what he had learned. It also sounded like he needed a lot of money to be able to pull it off, no matter what all the house flipping gurus said. When he looked into all the house-flipping programs he saw online, they all seemed to be about wholesaling and not house flipping anyway.

Wholesaling had interested him quite a bit, but he knew that would not be easy either. The idea was to find amazing deals, get them under contract, and then sell them to other investors, or at least sell the contract to other investors. He was not sure how all of that worked, but he knew he would have a lot to learn no matter what he pursued.

The other idea that had started to float around in his head lately was becoming a real estate agent or at least getting his real estate license. Mo still remembered the first day he saw Ryan and the $100,000 plus car he pulled up in. Ryan was a super cool guy and really nice, but there was no mistaking that he made a lot of money. If you are looking to make a lot of money, Mo thought it made sense to do what other people who had already made a lot of money did.

Mo also knew that becoming a real estate agent would be hard, but he could start out part-time as an agent or a wholesaler. Those did not seem to be things that he had to quit his job for. He was not ready to burn that bridge!

Mo ordered a few more books and found a few more blogs that focused on wholesaling and being a real estate agent. From the few things he had learned, it sounded like he would have to take classes and pass a test to be a real estate agent, but he would not have to do anything to be a wholesaler.

The one advantage that Mo really saw with being a real estate agent was he would save a ton of money whenever he bought or sold houses. Ryan made money when Mo would sell his houses, but if Mo was the agent, he could make that commission instead. He would also have access to the multiple listing service (MLS), where he could see the house listings from other agents in real time. He had some searches set up with Ryan and tried to find houses himself on sites like Zillow, but the listings were never updated, and many of them were already under contract when he tried to send a promising house to Ryan to look up.

There were a couple of blogs that had made being a real estate agent sound like an amazing idea for real estate investors and some other sites that said it was bad to be a real estate investor and real estate agent, especially if you wanted to wholesale houses. Mo was not sure what he wanted to do, but he knew he had to research a lot more. He was also fairly sure he would be putting the internet marketing thing on hold for the time being.

56

A decision?

Mo spent the next week going to work, doing the same old thing, going home, then reading. He would work out once in a while and watch some TV or a movie on occasion, but mainly, he was working and learning. He thought his life would seem boring to many people, but he was loving it. Every time he learned something new, he felt like he had accomplished something. He felt like he was expanding as a person and no one could ever take away that knowledge...unless someone hit him with a bus and he got amnesia, but he figured there was a pretty small chance of that happening.

Not much new happened at work. He talked to his boss Tory once in a while, but he never got any real training. They all seemed happy with how he was doing. He talked to Sarah a lot more, but he was super focused on himself at the moment. Mostly, he was learning what he wanted for the next chapter of his life. She seemed to be happy to take things slowly, but he knew he needed to include her on what was going on inside his head. He was making some huge decisions about his life, and it would be nice to bounce ideas off of someone.

He had learned a tremendous amount about about wholesaling and being a real estate agent. He was starting to lean towards one of those career paths. On the wholesaling side, he did not have to take any classes or pass a test. He could start finding deals, get them under contract, and find investors to sell those deals to. That sounded simple enough, but the execution did not seem as simple. In fact, he was reading a few sites that said the success rate of wholesalers was extremely low.

The problem with wholesaling that he saw was he had to find amazing deals. He most likely could not find houses on the MLS to wholesale. He had to send out postcards, drive around looking for crappy houses, or find other ways to find those deals. Then, once he found a deal, he had to convince the owner of the property to sell it to him at a very low price. He also had to somehow find a contract to write up and hope he did not commit any crimes in the process. Once he had the contract, he had to find buyers or other real estate investors who wanted to buy his deals. This was the business that he saw advertised all the time as a way to "flip" houses with no money. It was true you could get the house under contract without buying it, but you still needed money for marketing.

He also knew that many real estate investors made a ton of money wholesaling houses. While the success rate may not be very high, there were certainly a number of investors who seemed to be making a killing from the wholesaling business. Lamborghini also seemed to be doing very well because of real estate wholesalers. It seems like every wholesaler on Facebook had a Lambo.

Mo researched as much as he could about real estate agents as well. What he learned was that you had to take a lot of classes and pass a test, which was not a cake walk. You could not simply become a real estate agent after you passed the test. You then had to "hang" your license with a real estate broker. They were the head of real estate offices and hired agents to work under them. It seemed that the broker would determine how much the real estate agent got to keep of their commission. Most real estate agents worked solely on commissions. They only make money when they sell a house. In that way, real estate agents were very similar to wholesalers.

The real estate broker also kept part of the commission the real estate agent made on each sale and may charge fees above and beyond the commission split. There could be desk fees, transaction fees, fees for signs, etc. It seemed every real estate office had a different system for how they paid agents and the fees they charged them. The real estate agent would make a commission by either helping someone find a house to buy or helping someone sell a house they owned. Most people used real estate agents to buy or sell houses, and typically, the seller of a home pays the real estate agent commission. When wholesaling houses, real estate agents were usually not involved.

Mo learned that there are no set real estate commissions that agents charge buyers or sellers. However, he did see a few numbers that are used a lot, and HUD paid the buyer's agent and the listing agent 3% of the sales price. If Mo were to sell a house for $100,000, he would earn $3,000 under those numbers. Of course, he would have to pay some of that money to his broker as part of the commission split. The commission splits seemed to range from 50 to 100% for the agent with some companies. Mo wondered, in the beginning of his research, why every agent did not go with the company that paid the agents 100% of the commissions. He discovered that most agents do not succeed and quit the business because they do not sell houses. The companies that offer the lower split to agents claim to offer more training and have higher success rates.

Mo looked up how much money real estate agents made versus wholesalers, and he was very disappointed. Real estate agents seemed to make very little, especially at the beginning. He saw some stats that said agents make less than $15,000 their first year. That was crazy!

After a few years, the average salary climbed to $40,000 or more, but that was not enough to buy the sweet Audi S8 that Ryan had. There was some info about part-time agents bringing the averages down and most agents not being very good at their jobs, but Mo was still discouraged by those numbers.

When he tried to find out how much money wholesalers make, he found almost nothing. There were a few articles that talk about how rich you can be with very little money as a wholesaler, but there not any solid stats about averages.

Mo was still leaning towards being a real estate agent. He knew that many investors frowned up being an agent, but it seemed easier to get started. He could work in an office with people there to train him and help him learn the business. He was not sure, but he hoped to be able to start part-time while he still had his other job.

If he became a wholesaler, he was basically trying to figure out everything on his own or from an online course. He supposed he might be able to find a local wholesaler who would train him, but would they want to create more competition for themselves? He also liked the idea of saving money on the houses he bought because he was a real estate agent, and a few articles had said that being an agent also made it much easier to get more deals.

He was not sure yet, but getting his real estate license may be the next step for him.

Mo decided to let Sarah in on what he was working on. He asked her out on another date, and she quickly agreed. She mentioned something about wondering if they were going to go out again. Mo thought she was cool with his slowness, but maybe she was not quite as cool as he thought she would be.

57

It takes work

Mo knew he should have been paying more attention to Sarah, but he thought she was cool with whatever. That was obviously not the case, and he had not been working very hard to show her that he cared. He decided he needed to show the same gusto as their first date. He got her flowers again and showed up at her apartment. He said their destination was a surprise.

Mo took Sarah to a small amusement park that had putt putt, go carts, a small boat pond, and a few other activities. They ate junk food and had a great time. While they were having fun, Mo opened with Sarah about his life and why he had been a little distant lately. He talked about his job, whether he wanted to stay at the company, and all the different things going through his head. She was very receptive to everything he said, but she said something that took him aback.

"You know, we have talked about your life a lot, but you hardly know anything about me."

Mo was surprised at this remark...and embarrassed. He was embarrassed because he knew she was right. He had always fashioned himself as a gentleman, someone who cared about people and someone who listened to people. He was not that jerk on TV who only talked about himself and everyone watching the movie knew was completely wrong for the girl he was dating. Now he was that jerk. How did he let that happen?

He said, "You are right. With everything going on, I guess I have been a bit of a jerk. I do care about you. I care about what you do. I care about what you are thinking. I have been a bit obsessed with myself lately."

She responded to him with a little smile and said, "That is okay. I am glad you are man enough to admit it and didn't just storm off in an angry cloud of dust!"

He loved that she could be sarcastic in any situation. It did not matter how serious their talk was, she could relive some tension with a few well placed words. He told her, "So anyway I am really excited about my house and my career, and have you seen how awesome my car is?"

She started laughing and put her arms around him. She said, "You know that is the only reason I am here with you. It is not easy to find a guy with a ten-year-old Maxima."

He said, "Hey! It is only five years old, thank you very much." He was laughing too but stopped and asked her a serious question, "Okay, enough joking around. You are right that I am being a selfish jerk. So tell me what your goal at work is and what your aspirations are."

She must have been waiting for him to ask, because without hesitation she started right in, "You know I am an accountant. I love math and order. The job suits me well, but my aspirations in life do not end with me working in an insurance agency. I do have a plan."

Mo said, "Really? Well lets hear it!"

She kept going, "I took a job at the company to learn how they do things. I wanted to know how they manage people, how they hire people, how they pay people, and how they use accountants. My goal is to start my own company, and I figured the best way to learn how to do it was to work for another company and copy them."

Mo had a look of shock on his face

She responded, since he seemed to have a mouth full of mud and could not talk, "See, I told you you should stop talking about yourself. Other people can be interesting as well."

Mo did not know how to respond, but he did his best and said, "That is amazing. I had no idea that you were using the company to build a business. Someone had mentioned that you were jealous when I got promoted because you wanted to be a manager, but you want to be much more than that!"

Sarah said, "They were right, actually. I do want to be a manager, and I was slightly jealous of you. I have been at the company for years busting my balls, and they have never even hinted at a manager position. Then you half-ass your way into a management position after deciding to take your job seriously for a month."

Mo said, "If it makes you feel any better, my department is tiny, and being a manager is nothing to write home about. Your department is huge compared to mine, and the managers seem to have been here for decades."

Sarah responded, "You are right. It is much tougher to get a management position where I am, and most of the managers have a masters degree, which I do not. However, I could learn so much more about how the business runs as a manager."

Mo knew she was right, but he was not sure how to fix any of it. He said all he could think of, "Well, if I learn any amazing secrets, I will be sure to pass them on!"

They both had a great night, and Mo made an effort to talk about things besides himself. He had asked Sarah about his career and what she thought he should do, but she was not much help. She told him that it was not her place to tell him what to do with his life. That was something that he had to figure out. He supposed she was right.

58

Really? A blog?

Mo spent the next week reading about real estate agents and internet marketing. He felt a tug towards the marketing side, even after thinking getting his real estate license would be the best move for him. He still loved computers and thought there had to be a way to mix the computer side of him with the real estate side of things.

He thought he had developed a plan, and he was extremely excited to have some direction.

First, he needed to buy his house, get moved in, make some repairs, and live there for a year.

Next, he would start a blog that chronicled his adventures in real estate. The blogs had been the most helpful to him in learning, besides the books. He thought he could help other people while he wrote about his adventures and maybe even make a little side money along the way.

He would start taking real estate classes as soon as he could and work towards getting his license. It would take a while to get through the classes, pass the test, and find a broker, so he thought he should start sooner rather than later.

Mo knew he was taking on a lot at once, but he also had time on his side. He did not have a family yet, or even a girlfriend. He had a lot more time now that he did not party all time. He could make some serious headway into building up his life instead of waiting for life to come to him.

Mo was not sure exactly how his real estate investing, real estate agent, blogging, and day job would work together, but he knew he had to start somewhere. It felt amazing having some sort of plan to follow instead of being swallowed up by doubt what to do next. Mo figured that once he got more involved in all of these activities, he could figure out what to focus on and what steps to take at that point.

While Mo was taking on many things at once, he knew he had to be careful not to be too scattered. He had read a lot about focus and how it was important not to do too many things at once. Mo was not sure exactly what he was going to do yet or what to focus on, so he thought it was an okay move going for a few things at once. He knew he did not want to add wholesaling, flipping, and a bunch of other things to his plate until he had more direction.

Mo wanted to take action right away. He did not want to wait. He was thinking about how he could get started right away. He decided he did not need to wait to start his blog. It might even be more enjoyable for people if they saw his journey from before he bought his first house.

He signed up for a WordPress page to start his blog. He had no idea what to call his blog, but he had taken action, and it felt great.

Mo also looked for real estate schools. He found a decent online school for real estate classes. The classes were pricey, costing $1,000 for everything. He remember Ryan and Josie's advice not to buy anything until he bought his house. While he was tempted to pay for the courses and get started, he decided to wait to buy them until the house was officially his.

The next task was coming up—naming his blog.

59

Blogsestate

The next few weeks had gone by painfully slow as Mo waited for the closing date to come for his new house. He had been studying up on his new career paths and working at his job, but that did little to speed up the time. He was ready to get his house!

Mo had not come up with a great name for his blog yet, but he had written an article. He had written about how he had gotten started on his real estate journey while working his corporate job. It was not an amazing article, but he was proud he wrote it. He had not done much to promote it, so no one had really commented or said much about it. He had not even shared it on his Facebook page, as he was a little worried about what people would think of him. He tended to be a pretty low key guy and rarely, if ever, posted anything. He thought it might be a little messed up if the first thing he posted for a while was a self-promoting article, even if he had nothing to really promote except his blog.

While he had not come up with a great name, he had come up with something.

Blogsestate.com.

He was really not sure about the name. He wanted Blogestate.com, but it was already taken. Mo really wanted to mix real estate with blogging. He thought he was being clever until he realized someone else had the same idea. He saw that Blogsestate.com was available and jumped on it. He figured if he thought of a better name, he could change it later.

Mo was super excited because he was about ready to write his second article on the blog, which would be about buying his first house. He was set to close tomorrow!

His loan had been fully approved by Josie awhile back. He was mostly moved out of his apartment, with his stuff in a moving truck. He was sleeping on the floor in a sleeping bag. It was actually pretty fun.

He could not sleep very well, but it was not because of the hard floor. It was because he was excited and so close to his dream that he had started a few months ago. He knew nothing about real estate 6 months ago, and now he was buying a house. He was not buying just any house, but he was getting an awesome deal that he could eventually turn into a rental property. He felt like he was in a special club. He knew very few people ever invested in real estate, especially as young as he. It was not rocket science, and it did not even take that much money once he figured out how to do it.

He had some work ahead of him once he bought the house, as he planned to do much of the cosmetic work himself. He did not really know what he was doing, but he thought he could figure out how to paint a house. How hard could it be? He also had a plumber all lined up to fix the broken pipes so he could have water when he moved in. He was hoping the fix was simple.

The house had hardwood floors, which he would refinish eventually, but he was content to live with them for a while. He just had to tear out the carpet and clean. The house was definitely a little grungy, but again, Mo was fine with that, at least he hoped he would be until he could fix it up a little. He did not have the money to pay a contractor to come in and rehab everything, so he would have to be okay with taking it slowly.

The yard was also dead, and that made the house pretty ugly, but again, Mo could live with that. He did not think it would be too hard to revive the grass if he put copious amounts of water on it.

Mo had not yet bought his first house, but he felt like he was addicted to real estate already. He was so excited and knew this was the best possible move he could make financially. Even if the housing market tanked, he still had a place to live, and he still got an amazing deal. He would not have to sell the house if prices went down. He could keep making the payments and wait for the market to recover. The only real concern was losing his job, but even that might not be that bad.

Mo had done some research on what happens if you can't make your housing payments. Everyone makes it sound like the end of the world, but it almost sounds better than renting. For one, the bank cannot simply kick you out of the house if you stop making payments. They must foreclose on the house, which can take months or even years. When they foreclose on the house, the owner can keep living there for free. The bank makes the insurance payments, and they pay the property taxes to protect their investment. When the foreclosure process does move forward, most banks will pay the occupants to move out!

If Mo was renting his apartment and lost his job, the property management company could evict him within 30 to 45 days after he stopped paying rent. He might get one or two months of free living. They certainly were not going to pay him to move out. If he owned a house, he would get at least 6 months of free living, maybe more. Plus, he might get $1,000 or $2,000 to leave the place in decent shape. Yes, his credit would be ruined, but what better way to get back on your feet than a free place to live!

Mo was not hoping or planning to lose his house to foreclosure, but he had thought about the best and worst case scenarios when buying a home. No one could say he had not done his research!

Mo eventually went to sleep at about 2 a.m. when his excitement could not over power his exhaustion. Tomorrow would be the day he bought his first house!

60

You always remember the first time

Mo woke up early the next morning, even though he had not fallen asleep until 2. His internal alarm clock told him that something exciting was happening that day, and he needed to wake up!

As soon as he opened his eyes, he remembered that this was the day he would buy his first house. He had not gotten financial help from anyone, but he had gotten a lot of help from some really cool people he met along the way.

Mo had taken another vacation day since he had to miss some work for the 9 a.m. closing. He wanted to move as many things into his house as he could. He also needed to clear out his apartment and clean it up so he could get his full deposit back. Mo would not consider himself a clean freak, but he did not do any damage to his apartment, and it would look like it did when he moved in once he was done cleaning.

Mo showered, had some cereal, and got ready to go to the closing. He had already picked up the cashiers check he needed from the bank the previous day. He had to bring about $4,000 to the closing. He had already paid $1,000 for the earnest money when his offer was first accepted. He had to pay the 3.5% down payment and a few other costs that his 3% in seller-paid closing costs did not fully cover. He had a little money left in his checking account, but not much. If he had kept drinking and partying with his friends, there was no way he could have had enough money to buy the house.

He was also glad he did not buy the real estate classes because he had to pay a little more for the house than he was expecting. HUD has more costs than other sellers, and Mo knew this, but for some reason, he was underestimating how much money he would need. Mo would have to save up for a little longer before he could sign up for the classes. He also thought it was best he did not spend every single dime he had, and he would build up an emergency fund now that he had a house. He knew that some unexpected repairs could pop up.

The inspection and appraisal had not shown any major problems with the house, but that did not mean the stove, furnace, dishwasher, fridge, or something else could not break. He was used to the basic creature comforts at his apartment, and he did not want to have to be a barbarian and wash dishes in the sink.

Mo made sure to bring his check and his drivers license. Those were the two things that Ryan and Josie had told him not to forget! He collected his things and drove himself to the title company where the closing would take place.

He was a little impatient and ended up getting there ten minutes early. He was not quite sure what to expect at the closing. He thought there might be someone there from HUD, and he would meet the listing agent who worked for HUD. He was curious how it worked for that agent who got the HUD listings. Maybe Mo could do that one day...

The receptionist at the title company asked what Mo was there for, and he told her he was buying a house. She asked his name, and he told her.

She showed him to a conference room. After he declined anything to drink, he sat in a comfy leather chair and waited for the other people to show up.

Mo sat in the chair reminiscing about the process he had been through to get this house. He was going over in his head how it all started when Ryan walked in the room.

"Mo! You made it!" He exclaimed dramatically.

Mo replied, "Of course I made it. You think I would miss my first closing!"

Ryan grinned and said, "I meant that you made it to this point of buying your first house, not that you actually showed up. This is a big deal. This is what makes my job fun—seeing people achieve a dream, and many of them do not realize how big of a deal it is. It is special for me to help you because you worked so hard and spent so much time learning what you wanted. A lot of people just go with the flow and don't have a clue what is going on."

Mo said, "Well Ryan, I could not have done it without you. I met a few agents prior to meeting you at that open house. Let me say...they were less than impressive. Thank you for your help and guidance."

Ryan was about to respond when Josie and another lady walked into the room. Josie said hi to Mo, shook his hand, and she introduced him to Marilyn, who was the closer. Mo knew immediately he would not be able to remember that name.

Marilyn shook Mo's hand as well and asked for his ID. Mo gave her his ID and the check he'd been holding. She said she would make some copies really fast and be right back.

Ryan and Josie talked for a few minutes while Mo sat back in his chair and nervously waited for Marilyn. He asked Ryan if they had to wait for the HUD people, and Ryan told him that they rarely, if ever, showed up to closing. "HUD never shows up, but once in a blue moon, the agent for HUD will show up."

Marilyn came back in the room and asked Mo, "Are you ready to sign your life away?"

She laughed as if it was the funniest joke in the world, but Mo was not quite as amused.

Marilyn walked Mo through the closing while Ryan and Josie chit chatted away. Mo had to sign a lot of documents, and he had no clue about most of them. This was where he had to trust that the people he was working with were on his side.

Josie did go over the figures for Mo, which showed exactly what he was spending his money on. He had to pay for prepaid interest, insurance, title fees, closing fees, lender fees, flood fees, and a lot more stuff. It was a bit overwhelming, but Ryan reminded him that he was getting a smoking deal on this house, and it was well worth it. Mo relaxed, and as Marilyn had said, signed his life away.

After about 20 minutes of signing HUD documents, lender documents, and title documents, Mo was done. He had purchased a house. He had some apprehension because he did not understand half the things he signed. If he was being honest with himself, he had not understood 90% of what he signed. He still felt amazing. As Ryan had said earlier, he got a smoking deal.

After he was done signing, Josie gave Ryan a gift basket with some cheese, smoked meats, and crackers. Ryan gave him a gift card to

Home Depot. Ryan said, "Some people like to give frilly gifts. I like to give gifts you can use!" Mo was not expecting anything, so he was not complaining.

Ryan said, " I have another gift for you. HUD does not give us keys to the house. We have to have a locksmith change the locks for us. I have one waiting at the house, no charge to you. We can head over there right now, and I can give you the keys to your new house."

Mo was not sure what to say, so he gave Ryan a hug. "Thanks man, lets go!"

61

A new path

Mo Followed Ryan over to the house and was reminded the entire way how nice Ryan's Audi was. He wanted to talk to Ryan about his new motivation to become a real estate agent, but he was a little scared. He was not sure how Ryan would take it since Mo would be competition. Mo was sure Ryan would not care about the competition part, but Ryan would lose Mo as a client. And, Mo was pretty sure Ryan spent so much time and effort on this deal because he assumed Ryan would be a repeat customer with purchases in the future.

Right then, Mo had a thought that might make this work out for both Ryan and him. One of the real estate agent articles he had read mentioned new agents should try to join a team if possible. If a new agent could join a team, they might get more coaching, get help obtaining their license, and possibly make some side money as an assistant helping with the team.

Mo thought the team idea would be perfect for him since he had no clue how to make money with his real estate license and would need a lot of help! He was not sure if Ryan had a team or not, but if Ryan did not have a team, Mo thought maybe he could help him start one.

They arrived at the house, and Mo could not get rid of the giant smile on his face. Most people would not be nearly as excited as he was to buy this ugly house, but he loved it, not just because he had bought his first house, but because of what the house represented—all of his hard work, and all the potential for the future.

There was a truck in the driveway, and the locksmith was already working on re-keying the front door. Ryan told Mo that he had called the locksmith and told him to get started on the way over.

Mo decided this was as good as a time as any to break the news to Ryan.

"Thanks again for all your help. You really went above and beyond with me," Mo said. "I feel like I should be the one buying you gifts instead of the other way around."

Ryan replied, "No worries. I made a commission selling the house to you, and believe it or not, this is my job, In fact, this one commission may not seem like much, but helping someone like you buy a house will earn me much more than one commission. I may help you buy more houses, and I am guessing you will tell your friends and family to use me as well, which is how I sell the most houses. The better job I do for you, the more likely you are to tell other people about me. That is free advertising."

Now Mo really felt bad. Not only would Ryan not get any more deals from Mo, but if Mo became an agent, he could be the one helping his friends and family buy houses instead of Ryan. However, if he was able to work with Ryan in some way, he supposed Ryan would take a cut of what Mo sold. That would help Ryan out.

"I have an idea I wanted to run by you, Ryan. I have been trying to figure out my life, my career, and what I want to focus on for the future.

I love real estate, but it is not like I can quit my job and be a full-time real estate investor after buying one house."

Ryan said, "That makes sense. I would not expect that either. I thought you were pretty happy at your job though."

Mo replied, "It is a good job, and I have been happier there lately, but that is not what I want to do for the rest of my life. I have been looking hard at a lot of different options, and I think I came up with a plan."

"So what is it?" Ryan asked. "I feel like you are delaying a little bit."

"Well, I think I want to get my real estate license." Mo watched Ryan's face for any sign of delight, surprise or anger. He could not see much of a reaction, but Ryan seemed to be pondering the idea.

"That is really not a bad idea if you love real estate and houses. You have learned more about the business in a few months than just about anyone else I have worked with. I think that might be a good fit for you, but it won't be easy."

Mo replied, "I know it won't be easy. I saw the stats and know that most people fail at being an agent and make very little money in the beginning of their careers. I have been thinking about that as well, and I may have an idea that could help both of us."

Mo waited for Ryan to respond, but he was waiting for Mo to continue, so he did. "Do you have a team or any assistants that help you now?"

Ryan responded, "I don't have any direct assistants, but I have staff at the office who helps me and the other agents. They can write contracts, do marketing tasks, and help with many other things. I also have an agent who helps watch over my stuff when I go on vacation."

Mo thought that was the case, but he was not sure exactly how it worked with Ryan. "What if I became your assistant...or helped you start a team? I have thought about this a lot, and I would not expect you to do everything for me. As you can see, I am motivated, a self starter, and I have skills."

Ryan was looking at Mo with more interest, but Mo could see he was not sold on the idea yet. "What kind of skills?" Ryan asked.

Mo was on a roll now, and he was tempted to say he had computer hacking skills, but he refrained. "I am an expert at computers, and I have been learning a ton about internet marketing. I know you make a lot of your money from referrals and typical real estate activities, but what if I brought your marketing to another level? I can build you an awesome website, get your social media updated, and bring you more leads."

Ryan replied with a skeptical look on his face, "That sounds great, Mo, but I have tried the online lead sources before, and they tend to be a waste of money in my experience. I tried Zillow, Realtor.com, and a few other online marketing programs, and frankly, the leads sucked."

Mo was ready for this. He had not come unprepared to talk to Ryan. "I know they suck, and that is not at all what I am proposing. With Zillow and the other sites, you are competing with 5 other agents for a lead who will probably never buy a house from any of those agents. I am talking about organic leads who seek us out because of our marketing. The website will be created by us and geared towards local traffic. The social media will be the same way. Any lead that comes in will be yours—no competing with other agents."

"Yeah, but how much is all of this going to cost? I have been burned so many times from marketers in this business who have big promises and little results," Ryan replied.

Mo said, "Well, I can help you with any other tasks as well. I would even be willing to work as an intern for free if you help teach me how to be an agent." Mo was hoping he would still get paid, but this was something he wanted to offer in case Ryan had serious doubts. He added, "The social media will be virtually free unless we decide to advertise, but we do not have to do that. The website won't cost much at all either. I saw what you have now, and we can tweak it for now to make it work better."

Ryan thought some more and said, "You keep surprising me, I did not see this coming, and frankly, I don't know what to say at the moment. Tell you what...send me your resume, give me a proposal for what you want to do, and I will take a look at it all. If I decide this may work, we can talk more next week."

Mo smiled again and said, "That is all I wanted—a chance. I will get that together and wait to hear from you."

With that, Mo and Ryan walked through the house one more time and said their goodbyes. Mo was excited about a lot of things. Now he had to start moving, and later, he would try his best to impress Ryan with his proposal.

62

It feels like home

Mo spent the next two days moving his stuff into his new house. The only thing he did before moving in was rip out some of the carpet and throw it in the backyard. He had no idea what else to do with it, except throw it in the garage. However, he had never had a garage, and he made a promise to himself to keep it clean and leave enough room for his car.

After throwing the carpet outside, he cleaned thoroughly...well, as thoroughly as most guys clean he guessed. He had no idea how much dirt and dust there could be in and under the carpet and carpet pad. He also did not realize how heavy and awkward carpet was to carry.

He did not have a lot of things to move. He had his bed, a couch, some chairs, a small kitchen table, a desk, and a dresser. After moving his stuff in, the house still looked empty. He had no idea how he could make all the rooms seem somewhat lived in since most of them had nothing in them. He would worry about that later, as he had plenty of time to fix things up, and then he might buy some more furniture.

After moving everything over, he cleaned the apartment he had lived in for a few years. There were a few scuffs on the walls from a chair that rubbed on them or Mo carrying something a little carelessly, but he thought he would get his entire deposit back. He might miss his old apartment, but so far, he was happy to be out and in his new house.

Rob and Cory had helped Mo move some of the bigger stuff. They still talked once in a while, but they had not hung out since the last night at Robs apartment a few weeks back. They seemed genuinely happy for Mo, and Rob even hinted that he might try to buy a house in a couple of years. Mo was quick to mention that he might be able to help him out since he was planning to get his real estate license. Mo thought *you can never start marketing yourself too soon!*

They all hung out that first night, and Mo was happy to see them. They did not go crazy or go to the bars, although Mo thought Cory and Rob might have decided to go after they left his house. They had hinted about going earlier, but Mo was clear he didn't want to go anywhere but his new house that night.

Rob and Cory had mentioned that Mo had enough room to get a ping pong table, a pool table, foosball, darts, and just about any other game he wanted. Mo had missed playing games at the bars, but he had not missed all the drinking. He thought to himself that it might be fun to create a little bachelor pad for himself. He no longer had to worry about being too loud in his apartment, where his neighbors could hear just about everything he did.

Mo went to bed that night and could not believe how far he had come. He was back to having almost no money since he spent it all on the house. He had no renters to pay for the utilities or bills yet, and he was not making much more at work. However, he felt wealthier and richer after buying the house and knew that, eventually, it would be a great investment, even if it took a couple of years.

The next afternoon, he was working on the house when he got a text from Sarah. "Hey stud. Heard you bought a house....and have a Maxima."

He laughed to himself and texted her back, "You know it!" She knew he had the house and had even seen the house already. She had been with Mo when he did his final walk-through. The final walk-through allowed Mo to check out the house before he bought it to make sure everything was as it should be. With a HUD home, he just wanted to make sure a tree had not fallen on the house or it had not flooded. Ryan mentioned to Mo that on other deals, when the seller agrees to fix some things, the final walk-through allows the buyers to make sure everything was done.

She texted him back, "You might want to check your front porch."

Mo walked to the front door and opened it up. There she was standing on the front steps with some kind of plant. She said, "I figured you could use a housewarming, present so here you go."

They spent the rest of the afternoon and night hanging out, working on the house, and talking. It was awesome.

63

Don't take no

After Mo was settled in for a day and a half, he decided it was time to get to work—not his work where he was a pseudo manager, but work on his new career. He wanted to impress Ryan and make it impossible for him not to hire him. He was hoping he might even get paid a little bit when he was hired.

Ryan had asked for a resume. Mo had not messed with his resume for years. He found an old file on his laptop that said "resume" and opened it up. He was a little appalled and embarrassed when he looked at it. There were typos, almost no details, and it looked like the resume of someone who put as little effort as they could into creating it. Mo knew that was exactly what he had done. He thought he would get hired because he had a degree and was relatively good at talking to people. How important were resumes anyway?

Looking at his resume now, he was surprised he had been hired at all. The company he worked for must not have very high standards. Mo went to work adding details about his previous jobs and education, and he spent hours writing an introduction that explained the job he wanted and why he wanted it. He was not really sure if this was the best way to write a resume, but he felt it needed to be very specific to impress Ryan. It started out with,

"I am a very motivated and highly driven individual who seeks employment in a setting that will challenge me. I have mastered many technology skills and have management experience as well. I am a self-starter but am also great at following directions. The real estate industry is something I am passionate about, and I plan to obtain my real estate license to become a successful agent, no matter how long it takes or how many hours I have to work. To that end, I am able to apply my technical and marketing skills to a great company who is looking to grow while they nurture my career."

Mo was impressed with himself. He added all of his work history, education, and specific skills that he thought would help Ryan make the decision to hire him an easy one.

He was not done yet. Ryan had asked for a proposal as well. Mo figured he wanted an outline of what Mo planned to do to help his marketing. Mo had learned a lot about marketing in all his research, and he felt he had a decent idea on how to help agents get more leads and close more deals without spending a lot of money.

Mo knew a lot about Facebook, Instagram, and other social media sites. He had thought his insurance company could have used those marketing channels much better than they did, but Mo was not a marketer until recently. Actually, Mo remembered he had proposed to Tory the company spend some time on building a Facebook presence. His answer had been that it is the insurance agent's job to build a presence, not the companies job. Mo was not sure how that had made any sense, but he left the subject alone after that.

Mo had actually forgotten about that encounter until now. Maybe that was why he was so hesitant to propose any new ideas to Tory about improving the IT department. It did not matter to Mo much now because he was going to make his own career and not be hampered by an old-fashioned company that was intent on staying in the stone age.

Mo wrote a two-page proposal. He knew Ryan was a busy guy and would not want to read a book. Mo highlighted how he could grow his followers with more posts, more pictures, a few tweaks to his website, and in the future, some paid advertising if things went well. The cost to Ryan would be almost nothing, unless he decided to pay Mo, which Mo was really hoping for. Mo also made it very clear that he could handle almost all the work, but Ryan would have to provide some content for him to post, like pictures. If Ryan was willing to do a video or two, that would be a huge bonus.

Mo ended the proposal by mentioning the role Ryan would play in Mo's development as an agent. Mo had not said anything to Ryan about possible commission splits or how he would be paid, if he was paid. He wanted to be clear that he was not doing this out of the goodness of his heart. It could be a win/win situation for both of them, but Mo did not want to work for free and get nothing out of the deal either.

Mo said that while he was helping Ryan with his business, Ryan would be a mentor. Mo would expect to go on showings, expect Ryan to show him how the MLS works and help him learn how to value properties, and anything else he needed to know as an agent. Mo finished the proposal by saying that he envisioned a situation where they worked together off each other's strengths. Ryan would show Mo how to be a great agent, and Mo would help Ryan grow his business without breaking the bank on marketing costs. Eventually, Mo could help Ryan with other real estate tasks as well once he got licensed.

Mo did not ask Ryan to pay for his license or mention any compensation in his resume or the proposal. He wanted Ryan to say yes, and then they could work out the details. Sarah reviewed everything and pointed out a few things to change and a couple of typos.

Ryan was ready.

64

Are you up for it?

Ryan texted Mo, and they set up a time to meet at Ryan's office the next week. Mo had missed a fair amount of work and was thankful that Ryan was willing to meet him for lunch one day.

They met at a restaurant close to Mo's work because Ryan knew Mo did not have the flexible schedule that he had. They sat down with a bit of tension between the two as they said their hellos. Mo did not want to waste any time and got right to the point.

"Ryan, I put together the proposal you asked for, and I have my resume here. I am dead serious about working with you, and I hope it shows in what I have done here. I did not take it lightly, and I will not take working with you lightly if you choose to do this."

Mo handed Ryan the two documents and waited for him to look them over. Ryan read over his resume fairly quickly and then read through the proposal. He read through that fairly quickly as well. He looked at Mo and said, "What is your timeline for becoming an agent?"

Mo said quickly, "I want to become one right away, as soon as I finish my classes and take the test."

Ryan responded with, "Yes, I hear that a lot from people who want to be agents, but how long will that take? A couple of months? A couple of years?"

Mo was a little worried. He thought he had gone over everything in his head, but he had not thought about exact timelines for when all of this would happen. He considered making up some numbers but decided to be honest, "To be honest, I had not thought about the exact timeline for obtaining my license. I guess, in my head, I was thinking it would be a few months, but I have not gone over exactly what I have to do. I just know I want to do it, and I will get it done. "

"Okay," Ryan replied, "What about your job? Are you going to keep working there forever, or have you thought about when you will leave that and be a full-time agent?"

Damn, Mo thought to himself. He had put all this work into impressing Ryan, and he was realizing how many questions he had not answered for himself, let alone for Ryan, "I definitely do not plan to work there forever. I want to be a full-time agent, but I do not know how long it will take me to make a decent living. I was thinking it might be a year until I was ready to go full time."

Ryan considered this and responded, "I am sure you have researched being an agent and know that most part-timers do not do well. It is really hard to make money as an agent when you have another job. One way to be more successful as a part timer is to work on a team, but it is still tough. The sooner you break it off with that company, the sooner you will succeed as an agent."

Mo was worried now. Had he really screwed all this up? "I did read that about part-time agents. I should have thought about timeframes more. I guess I was so focused on showing how I could help you that I forgot about some really important points."

Ryan smiled, "Don't worry, Mo. I think you will do just fine, and we can figure that out when the time comes. I did not expect you to have this all figured out after two days. I have interviewed a few agents or potential agents who wanted to work with me, and none of them came close to preparing like you did. They all assumed they could just show up and I would tell them how to 'make bank.' You came with a plan and a way to help me, which makes sense. Although, the tech side is tough for me given my limited knowledge on marketing and my age."

Mo laughed and felt a wave of relief flow over him. Ryan was not that old, but he was older than Mo. Maybe he had not screwed up! "Does this mean I get to work with you? I mean, for you?"

Ryan responded, "Yes, I think we should be able to work something out. I might even pay you a little bit, even though you offered to work for free. I won't pay for your license now, but if you pass the test, I will pay for half your license costs when you sell your first house."

Mo could not help himself. He blurted out, "Deal!" and shook Ryan's hand. He was ecstatic and knew he was on to something big.

Ryan and Mo finished their lunch and would meet later in the week to iron out the details. Ryan knew that Mo would be working part time in the evening and weekends. He told Mo he was not expecting a miracle on the marketing side but would want detailed updates and reports on how things were going. He also told Mo that if he was dishonest with him, he would fire him immediately. He could work with a lot of faults, but lying was not one of them.

Mo watched Ryan get into his car. He could not believe he had pulled that off. He had a new house, a new job, possibly a new career, and a promising relationship. This was a good day, and he could not wait to see what the future held for him.

The end.

About Mark Ferguson

I have been a licensed real estate agent/broker since 2002. My father has been a Realtor since 1978, and I was surrounded by real estate in my youth. I remember sleeping under my dad's desk when I was three while he worked tirelessly in the office. Surprisingly—or maybe not—I never wanted anything to do with real estate. I graduated from the University of Colorado with a degree in business finance in 2001. I could not find a job that was appealing to me, so I reluctantly decided to work with my father part-time in real estate. So many years later, I am sure glad I got into the real estate business!

Even though I had help getting started in real estate, I did not find success until I was in the business for five years. I tried to follow my father's path, which did not mesh well with me. I found my own path as an REO agent, and my career took off. Many people think I had a huge advantage working with my father, and he was a great help, but I think that I actually would have been more successful sooner if I had been working on my own, forced to find my own path.

Now I own a real estate brokerage. I fix and flip 20-30 houses per year, and I own 20 long-term rentals. I love real estate and investing because of the money you can make and the freedom running your own business brings.

I started InvestFourMore (a blog) in March 2013 with the primary objective of providing information about investing in long-term rentals. I was not a writer at any time in my life until I started this blog. In fact, I had not written anything besides a basic letter since college. Readers who have been with me from the beginning may remember how tough it was to read my first articles, with all the typos and poor grammar (I know it still isn't perfect!). My goal has always been to provide incredible information, not to provide perfect articles with perfect grammar.

The name "InvestFourMore" is a play on words, indicating that it is possible to finance more than four properties. The blog provides articles on financing, finding, buying, rehabbing, and renting out rental properties. The blog also discusses mortgage pay down strategies, fix and flips, advice for real estate agents, and many other real estate related topics.

I live in Greeley Colorado, which is about 50 miles North of Denver. I married my beautiful wife Jeni in 2008, and we have twins who were born June of 2011. Jeni was a Realtor when we met in 2005 but has since put her license on ice while she takes care of the twins. Jeni loves to sew and makes children's dresses under the label Kaiya Papaya.

Outside of work, I love to travel, play golf, and work/play with my cars.

Want to Learn More?

If you enjoyed this book and are interested in learning more about real estate, you may be interested in my other books:

- How to Build a Rental Property Empire

- Fix and Flip Your Way to Financial Freedom

- How to Buy a House

- How to Make it Big as a Real Estate Agent

- The Book on Negotiating Real Estate (co-written with J Scott)

- How to Change Your Mindset to Achieve Huge Success

I also write new articles on my blog https://investfourmore.com all the time and have many resources for investors and agents on the site. I have hundreds of videos on the InvestFourMore YouTube channel as well. We shoot videos of just about every house we buy, and I have been buying close to or more than 30 properties a year the last few years. You can also follow me on the InvestFourMore Instagram or Facebook page where we post daily.

41662346R00158

Made in the USA
Lexington, KY
09 June 2019